"Loathe me all you like. That doesn't mean you don't want me."

"Want you? I'd sooner want a snake."

"Yeah?"

"Yeah."

"Well, considering what was going on here a little while ago, you're going to make some snake a very happy reptile."

Susannah swung toward him, her hands knotted into fists. Any second now, she was going to lose her chance at *Chic* magazine, probably her chance at anything, because once she slugged the horrible Matt Romano, what would be her chance of getting another job in publishing?

"You really do think you're the sexiest man alive, don't you? Well, let me tell you something, Romano. Just because I was stupid enough to let you kiss me—"

Dear Reader,

What makes you happiest on Valentine's Day? A heart-shaped box of chocolates? A dozen long-stemmed roses? I always thought those things were perfect celebrations of love. Then, one Valentine's Day a couple of years ago, a winter storm raced through our part of New England. It buried the countryside in snow, took out our electricity and ruined our plans for dinner at a wonderful old inn. Instead, my husband and I bundled up in long underwear, jeans and sweaters. He lit a fire on the hearth, I grilled hamburgers and we opened a bottle of wine. We turned on the portable radio and danced to some old love songs. An elegant Valentine's Day? No. But it was the most romantic one I've ever spent, and I'll never forget it.

Love,

Sandra Marton

Write to Sandra Marton at:
P.O. Box 295
Storrs, CT 06268
SandraMarton@worldnet.att.net

SANDRA
MARTON

The Sexiest Man Alive

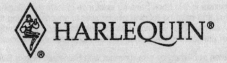

TORONTO • NEW YORK • LONDON
AMSTERDAM • PARIS • SYDNEY • HAMBURG
STOCKHOLM • ATHENS • TOKYO • MILAN • MADRID
PRAGUE • WARSAW • BUDAPEST • AUCKLAND

ISBN 0-373-12008-7

THE SEXIEST MAN ALIVE

First North American Publication 1999.

PROLOGUE

●

CHIC

Today's Magazine for Today's Woman
Edgar B. Elerbee, Publisher
from the desk of: Edgar B. Elerbee
to: Editorial Staff
Tuesday, June 3

It is with great sorrow that I announce the sudden passing of Charles Dunn, our esteemed editor-in-chief. Charles was the guiding force of this publication for 32 years, and I know our entire staff will miss him.

Effective immediately, I am naming our managing editor, James Colter, to succeed Charles in this most important role. I expect the entire staff to join me in offering James our complete support.

E. Elerbee, pub.

●

from: ClaireHaines@chic.com
to: SusannahMadison@chic.com
subj: Major Surgery needed

Suze: I guess old Charlie put in one garter-belt-and-blindfold weekend too many. But Colter? Yuck. Charlie never understood the 20th century woman, but Colter probably thinks we should still be wearing bustles. Lunch at Gino's? We can have pasta and whine.

•

from: SusannahMadison@chic.com
to: ClaireHaines@chic.com
subj: Getting Trampled in the Rush for the Door

Elerbee's got to be kidding! Our circulation numbers were bad enough under Charlie, but Colter's going to set new lows. Hasn't it ever occurred to Elerbee that a mag for women ought to have a woman at its helm? Forget Gino's. I went home this weekend. My mother baked up a storm. I should have saved time & put the stuff right on my hips.

•

Suze:
Size eights don't have hips to worry about!
Demos you requested attached. Readers are women 40-65. Not target group. Not good news. Heard the latest dirt? Colter is history. Wonder who Elerbee will put in his place?
Claire

•

from: SusannahMadison@chic.com
to: ClaireHaines@chic.com
subj: Mister Ed, The Talking Horse

Or maybe Lassie. But not anyone who could breathe some life into CHIC. You're right. Demographic breakdown is N.G. Women, single, 18-35. That's where we should be aiming. We need more picture spreads, more fashion stuff, makeup ideas, advice on men. I've had it with Mom, apple pie and babies. What ever happened to the joys of being a single woman???

●

from: ClaireHaines@chic.com
to: SusannahMadison@chic.com
subj: Single Women, 18-35
The lucky ones got married.

●

from: SusannahMadison@chic.com
to: ClaireHaines@chic.com
subj: Definitions
Depends on your definition of ``lucky.''

●

from: ClaireHaines@chic.com
to: SusannahMadison@chic.com
subj: Cold Feet
A career doesn't keep you warm at night.

●

from: SusannahMadison@chic.com
to: ClaireHaines@chic.com
subj: Cures for Cold Feet
Try an electric blanket. Or get a cat.

●

from: ClaireHaines@chic.com
to: SusannahMadison@chic.com
subj: Women can Purr, Too
You're heartless, Madison.

•

from: SusannahMadison@chic.com
to: ClaireHaines@chic.com
subj: Better a Cat than a Kitten
I'm practical, Haines.

•

CHIC
The Magazine for Women
Edgar B. Elerbee, Publisher
July 28
Please join me at a buffet breakfast in the boardroom
Friday, from 8:30 to 10, in honor of our new editor-in-
chief, Julius Partridge Wallinger. Mr. Wallinger brings
with him almost 40 years of journalistic know-how.
Payroll has asked me to assure you that the problem
with last week's checks was computer related and will
not occur again. Thank you for your forbearance.
E. Elerbee, pub.

•

from: SusannahMadison@chic.com
to: ClaireHaines@chic.com
subj: Hello
Enjoying vacation. Weather is glorious.
Relaxing on all sides. Reading, renting vid-
eos, etc. Old friend's been coming around—
Sam. Did I ever mention him? My ever-hopeful
Mom invites him for dinner each night, which
makes me smile. Sam's a sweetheart. He plays
canasta with her after I go to bed.
Saw an item buried in back of Business Daily.
Is it true? Has the new guy gotten the boot
already? I've only been on vacation a week!!!
What about rumor of a Romano Inc takeover? Not

really possible, is it? I spotted him in
Hyannisport. (Drove there to treat Mom to
lunch.) The only thing Matthew Romano could
do for CHIC would be to let the mag lay him out
as a centerfold... Not that any intelligent
woman would find the studly-but-brain-
lessly-arrogant Mr. Romano a turn-on. He was
with Ted Turner. Now, there's a guy I'd love
to see buy CHIC. Tell Peter I send love &
kisses, & that I miss him.

•

MEMO

FROM: Claire
TO: Claire

1. Remember to ask S. about Sam, & why he's playing cards with Mom instead of romancing S.
2. Remember not to bother asking.
3. Remember to ask how come she took portable computer on vacation.
4. Remember not to bother asking.
5. Remember to suggest S. should toss her hat in the ring for next ed-in-chief hiring go-round. She has an MBA , hasn't she?
6. Remember above, for sure. S. would make great ed-in-chief.
7. Remember to tell S. the Romano thing is nothing but an off-the-wall rumor.
8. Remember to ask S. how she knows Romano is brainless, arrogant & studly. (Studly??? Susannah, how you do talk.)
9. Tell S. she's got a way with a phrase. "Laying out" Romano, that hunk, is a wonderful idea.

•

from: SusannahMadison@chic.com
to: ClaireHaines@chic.com
subj: Tossed Hats & Studs

OK, I did it. I gave Elerbee my résumé. He didn't laugh... I guess that's good news. Re Matthew Romano & layouts: Claire, where are your standards? Who wants a guy who thinks he's the sexiest man alive? Only a DB, like the one who was draped across Romano's arm at Hyannisport.

•

from: ClaireHaines@chic.com
to: SusannahMadison@chic.com
subj: Sexiest Man Alive? DB?

When? How? What? Explain, please.

•

from: SusannahMadison@chic.com
to: Claire Haines@chic.com
subj: When, How, What

DB=Dumb Blonde, as always seen in tabloid photos of Romano. Sexiest Man Alive, as seen in Romano's smirk in every tabloid shot.

•

from: ClaireHaines@chic.com
to: SusannahMadison@chic.com
subj: Confusion

For shame, Suze. Didn't know you read the tabloids (snicker). And how do you know the Bs are D?

●

from: SusannahMadison@chic.com
to: ClaireHaines@chic.com
subj: No Confusion
Romano was with them.

●

from: ClaireHaines@chic.com
to: SusannahMadison@chic.com
subj: Yes, Confusion
How come you're so interested in Matthew Romano?

●

from: SusannahMadison@chic.com
to: ClaireHaines@chic.com
subj: Non-Interest
I'm not. I don't know how we got off on this subject to start with.

●

from: ClaireHaines@chic.com
to: SusannahMadison@chic.com
subj: Confused, Again
You said he was studly.

●

from: SusannahMadison@chic.com
to: ClaireHaines@chic.com
subj: Insanity
Good grief! I was being sarcastic! Why are we wasting time on this man?

•

from: ClaireHaines@chic.com
to: SusannahMadison@chic.com
subj: Hey!
It wasn't me who brought Romano the Stud into
the conversation.

•

You're right. I did—and I'm taking him out of it, now.
Do me a favor. Take a look at attached: tell me what you
think of these ideas. Would any of them make you, for
instance, buy a copy of CHIC?
Uh-oh. Phone call from Elerbee. Wants to see me pronto.
Here comes the turn-down...

•

CHIC
The Magazine for Tomorrow's Woman
Edgar B. Elerbee, Publisher

I am delighted to announce that Susannah Madison
is our new editor-in-chief. Susannah has been with us
as senior editor for the past two years. She'll be assuming her new post at the start of next week. I know you've
weathered some difficult moments the last few months
but I can assure you, that's all behind us.

The payroll dept. has asked me to inform those who
may have, again, experienced some difficulty cashing
last week's checks to please be patient. The problem is
computer related. Thank you again for your forbearance
and, may I add, it's been a pleasure working with all of
you these past years.

E. Elerbee

●

from: Susannah Madison, editor-in-chief
to: Staff
I have just been informed that CHIC has been
purchased by Update Publications of NYC.
Don't panic, people. I'm trying to get info
re Update. As soon as I do, I'll cc: whatever
I have to all of you. Since we've never heard
of it, it's probably a small outfit, one that
will give us time to regroup, retrench & make
CHIC the winner we all know it can be.
Susannah

●

While You Were Out
Mr. E:
S.M. phoned. Asked for info re rumors sale of
magazine. What shall I tell her?
Pam

●

from: ClaireHaines@chic.com
to: SusannahMadison@chic.com
subj: Congrats & Query
Wow! Congratulations, Suze. You'll be great!
What's Elerbee mean, ''It's been a pleasure,'' etc. Is he retiring? Selling? The mag
can't be going under, not if he's just ap-
pointed you ed-in-chief, right? RIGHT??

•

MEMO

from: Matthew Romano
to: Joseph Romano
re: CHIC takeover
Sept 10
Joe:
Update Division just acquired CHIC as part of the Elerbee package. From what I've seen, the kindest thing would be to put it out of its misery. What in hell's going on there? I want to see some data. Copies of correspondence re revolving-door ed-in-chief position, also any pertinent correspondence, files, email, etc on my desk, ASAP.
Matt

•

from: JoeRomano@romano.com
to: MattRomano@romano.com
subj: Some guys are, some guys aren't
Thanks a lot, big brother. You just about kept me chained to my desk this weekend. Info on its way. Files sent via Internet, pertinent correspondence faxed. Emails mostly office chitchat—but you should take a look at some of them. Forwarding same to your acct. Got to say, buddy, I never did notice you were (ahem) studly.
Joe (trying very hard not to guffaw)
P.S. I guess I'd better tell you now, I'm not the only one who eyeballed this stuff. Material went thru a few hands before hitting my desk. Sorry, but you have to admit, it's funny.

●

MEMO

from: Matthew Romano
to: Jane
re: Elerbee package

Jane:
Will be leaving for NY on Sun. Contact Hank. Tell him I'll need the plane. Arrange for hotel accommodations. Also phone CHIC offices, inform ed-in-chief I'll expect to see her in her office 9 AM Monday.
MR

Jane—Flowers to Miss Darvis, please. A dozen roses. Make it two dozen. Apologies, etc. for breaking next Sun night engagement. Tell her I'll phone from NY. As for ed-in-chief…please be sure to impress upon the lady that she'd damn well better be prompt.

●

from: MattRomano@romano.com
to: JaneTrent@romano.com
subj: CHIC

I've changed my mind. Do not contact ed-in-chief at CHIC. I prefer to make my visit unannounced.

CHAPTER ONE

SUSANNAH stepped from the shower, wrapped herself in a towel and raced down the chilly hallway to the kitchen.

This day—this very important day—was not off to a good start.

The shower had been so cold it had made her teeth chatter. The radiators were rattling enough to wake the dead, but the heat trickling out of them wouldn't have heated a dollhouse. And, as she set the kettle on to boil, a cockroach the size of Godzilla scurried across the linoleum.

But it was what she read on the clock over the stove that set her heart pounding.

Seven-fifteen?

It couldn't be. No way. It was six-fifteen, it had to be. She'd set her alarm an hour earlier than usual, given herself more than enough time to get dressed, put on her makeup and blow-dry her hair, have a slice of toast with her coffee, make Peter his breakfast and still arrive at the office before anyone else.

It was important to seem cool, calm and collected when she started today's meeting, and never mind that her heart would be in her throat. Even the fortune cookie that had come with last night's order of take-out General Tso's chicken had said that much.

Tomorrow, the little slip of paper in the cookie had promised, *is the first day of the rest of your life.*

Well, of course it is, the practical little voice in Susannah's head had whispered, but the other voice, the one that lived in her heart or her soul or wherever it was hopes and prayers lived, that voice had said, *You see, Susannah? The whole world knows that you're standing on the edge of your dream.*

Editor-in-chief. Not in five years, or ten, but right now. A giant step up the ladder. A Career, capital C, and all that went with it—independence, respect and security. That was

16

the dream. Now, long before she'd ever imagined it would happen, she had her shot at achieving it. And she wasn't going to be shoved off course by a malfunctioning kitchen clock.

The clock was definitely broken, that was all there was to it. She'd set her alarm, it had gone off...and if she needed any further proof that it was after six, not after seven, all she had to do was take a look at Peter, who was still lying asleep in her bed.

Susannah gave a sigh of relief. That was something, anyway. The last thing she needed right now was to have to deal with Peter's early-morning grumpiness. He was gorgeous, and she adored him, but there were times you had to tiptoe around his ego. He was, typically, disgustingly, arrogantly male.

Well, no. Mr. Matthew Romano, he of the smug smiles and the decorative blondes, *he* was typically male. Peter, on the other hand, could be a sweetheart when he wanted to. And he understood that her life could not revolve around him. He didn't complain if she worked late or expect her to put her career on hold so she could be there to take care of his needs.

"It's because he doesn't really love you, Suze," Claire had said more than once.

But he did, in his own way. He put what he could into the relationship, which was undoubtedly more than could be said of someone like Matthew Romano....

What on earth was wrong with her this morning? Why was she wasting precious time thinking about a man she'd never even met?

"Ridiculous," she said.

Ridiculous, indeed. There was absolutely no reason for the insufferable Mr. Romano to wander through her thoughts, but this was the second or third time it had happened since she'd seen him on the Cape. Actually, it had been equally ridiculous for her to have taken such an instant dislike to him. It was just the way he'd strutted along with the blonde on his arm and that smug, I-am-the-world's-gift-to-womankind smile on his face.

Positively insufferable.

She'd never even have noticed him if she hadn't been thinking about *CHIC* and about publishing. There was Ted Turner, who everybody knew was brilliant and who looked like a nice guy, and then, by contrast, there was Matthew Romano, who'd probably never done anything more difficult in his life than play with his money and his groupies, looking as if he figured every woman on the planet wanted his body.

Not that it was a bad-looking body.

Susannah frowned and plucked her watch from the dresser. By now, it should be just about a quarter after six....

Oh God.

Her stomach tumbled to her toes.

Mickey Mouse grinned at her, one white-gloved, four-fingered hand pointing at the number four, and the other...

The other pointed straight at seven.

She tossed the bath towel across the room. It soared through the air and onto the bed, landing, with a dreadful accuracy, on Peter's head.

"No," she whispered, but it was too late. Peter came awake in a flash, bristling with anger. He shot to his feet and glared at her through cold green eyes. "Peter. Oh, Petey, sweetheart, I didn't mean..."

Whether she'd meant it or not didn't matter. Peter didn't believe in apologies. He never had, not since the day he'd come into her life. She watched as he turned his back on her and stalked from the room.

"Do your thing, Peter," she muttered. "I couldn't care less. I've got more important things to worry about this morning than you and your attitude."

Peter muttered something out in the hall, but Susannah paid no attention. She was going to be late. Later than late, and on this, the first day of the rest of her life.

Well, it was.

She was holding the very first meeting she'd ever called at *CHIC*, the first she'd oversee as its editor-in-chief. That was the good news. The bad was that the meeting might be her last, unless this morning's brainstorming session ended in some wild and wonderful idea that would make the brass from Update Publications decide their latest acquisition was worth keeping alive. Otherwise, *CHIC* and the biggest chance she'd ever had in her career, along with all the magazine's staffers, were going to be flushed out to sea.

Susannah threw another harried glance at her watch as she pulled on her jeans.

Seven twenty-four. If she got out of here in the next ten minutes—make that eight minutes—she had a chance. All she had to do was put on a shirt, her sneakers, find the notes she'd worked on all weekend, dump them into her handbag...

Peter yelled.

All she had to do was finish dressing, get her stuff together, give Peter his breakfast, and she'd be on her way.

She yanked a Beethoven's Got the Beat T-shirt over her head. Droplets of water flew from her short black curls. She shrugged impatiently and tunneled her fingers through her hair. Forget about the luxury of blow-drying. Forget about toast, or even coffee. Forget about everything but the meeting. Assuming the subway trains weren't running late, assuming the construction mess around Third Avenue had been cleaned up, assuming all was right with the world, maybe, *maybe,* she could make it into the office on time.

She had to.

On Friday, she'd laid down the rules for today's conference. She'd done it not by E-mail or interoffice memo—it was too important for that. Instead, she'd told her secretary to phone each person in the *CHIC* organization, from Eddie the mail-room boy...

"Eddie, the mail-room intern," Pam had said, raising her eyebrows.

"I don't care if he's Eddie, the mail-room CEO," Susannah had answered. "Just make sure he and everybody else knows I want them assembled in the boardroom today at ten minutes to five."

They'd straggled in, which she'd expected. *CHIC* was casual when it came to dress, something that was pretty common in the publishing world, but now, thanks to the revolving-door editor-in-chief policy, some of the staff had an attitude of indifference that verged on apathy. Her staffers had crowded into the room with their containers of coffee, their cans of diet cola, and once they were all there, Susannah held up her hands for quiet.

"Here's the deal," she'd said briskly. "It's just a matter of time before this Update outfit decides to take a closer look at us. When they do, we'd better be ready to dazzle 'em with facts and figures and plans for the future so they leave thinking that *CHIC* is an eagle, ready to fly—instead of a dying swan that needs to be shot to put it out of its misery."

"I don't think they do that to swans," the features editorial assistant had said, but she was shushed to silence.

"I want you all to go home and think about what we need to do to kick start this magazine into the twenty-first century," Susannah had continued. "And then I want you to show up here Monday morning, ready with innovative projects that will work, not just ideas that are impractical and expensive. And I want you all here promptly at eight."

There were grumbles and protests, but Susannah had stood firm.

"Look at it this way, people," she'd said. "If we're not ready with an A-number-one plan when Update comes in, we might as well figure on convening our next meeting at the unemployment office."

That had stopped the protests. *CHIC*'s staffers had filed out of the boardroom looking unhappy but determined.

"Eight sharp," Claire had said, and Susannah had nodded. "Exactly," she'd replied.

The big hand on the twelve. The little hand on the eight. Eight exactly. Not eight oh-five, or eight-ten. Eight.

Susannah puffed out her breath. There was nothing like setting a good example for the troops.

Okay. Zip up the jeans. Fluff up the hair one more time so maybe it wouldn't dry plastered to her head. Pull on socks, tuck feet into sneakers, tie laces...

Tear lace on right sneaker in half.

Easy. She had to stay calm. There had to be another pair of laces somewhere in the room. In the dresser drawers. In the closet...

There wasn't. Susannah said a word that would have made her grandmother blush. She grabbed two safety pins from the top drawer, hooked them through the eyelets on the sneaker, linked them together and closed them.

Then she stood and looked in the mirror.

Oh, boy.

No makeup. A hairdo that would have brought tears to the eyes of her hairdresser. A T-shirt that had a bleach spot on the sleeve and jeans that had really seen better days.

There was no sense even thinking about the safety pins and the sneaker.

Nevertheless, she was ready, and wasn't it a good thing that *CHIC* was so casual, because if she'd had to put on panty hose and iron a blouse, pick out a suit, buff a pair of pumps, put on makeup and jewelry and fix her hair, it would be noon before she got herself out the door.

As it was, Mickey was already pointing his white-gloved hand at...

Oh, hell.

Susannah raced from the bedroom and nearly collided with Peter, who was waiting for her in the middle of the hall. He opened his mouth, but she didn't give him the chance to say anything.

"I know, I know. You're starved. You're famished. And you're incapable of doing a thing about it without my help."

Peter sat down, his green eyes fixed on her as she banged open the cabinet over the stove.

"Sardine Soufflé," she said. "How's that sound?"

Peter yawned.

"Salmon Surprise? Bacon Bordelaise? Mmm, mmm, good."

Peter scratched his ribs.

"Tuna," Susannah said through her teeth. "You love tuna, Petey. You know you do."

Peter looked toward the window. Susannah could have sworn she heard him whistling.

"All right," she said grimly. "You win. Lobster and Shrimp Ragout, and you'd better remember this moment, Peter, because now you owe me one."

Peter turned and looked at her. "Meowr," he said in the sweetest voice any Persian pussycat had ever possessed. He jumped gracefully onto the counter and butted his furry head against Susannah's chin.

"Yeah, yeah, yeah," Susannah said wearily, but she smiled and kissed him right between his silky ears.

Whatever else happened today, at least she had Peter to come home to.

The view from Matthew Romano's suite in the new and elegant Manhattan Towers Hotel was, the concierge had assured him on checking in, spectacular.

"Spe-tac-u-lair, Monsieur Romano," was actually what the guy had said, in a gurgling French accent Matthew suspected to be about as legitimate as the Rolex watches hawked on the sidewalk a couple of streets over, but Matthew had nodded politely and said he was delighted to hear it.

The truth was, he didn't much care about the view. A man who'd built what the experts had taken to calling an empire in less than ten years was a man who spent a lot of time in hotel rooms. The rooms had improved as the Romano holdings had grown, but a hotel was still a hotel. Spe-tac-u-lair views, chilled Dom Pérignon, baskets of flowers and gold-plated bathroom fixtures couldn't change that one whit.

Whatever a whit might be, Matthew thought, as he stood gazing out the window of his sitting room. It was still early, just a little past seven, but traffic already clogged Fifth Avenue. Back home in San Francisco, most people would still be asleep…most people, but not the ones who earned their living from the sea.

There were times he was still amazed that he wasn't one of them. It was an honest way to make a buck but, even as a boy, he'd always suspected there was more to life. He hadn't wanted to begin his day while the rest of San Francisco slept or to pull on clothes that smelled of crabs and fish and sweat no matter how many times you washed them. And he sure as hell hadn't wanted to work his butt off for barely enough money to pay the bills.

It was what his father had done, and his grandfather. It was what he'd been expected to do, too.

The smile vanished. Matthew straightened, thrust his fingers through his dark hair and turned his back to the window and to the memories.

All that was years behind him. He worked his butt off,

yes, but he loved every minute of what he did. Someday, maybe, he'd want more. A wife. A family.

But not yet.

When he was ready, he'd find himself a wife. He knew exactly the kind of woman she'd be. Beautiful, of course, and serene. Eager to please. He could see himself coming home to her at night, kissing her, leaving behind the rough-and-tumble of business as he settled into his easy chair.

His wife would be a calm haven in the stormy seas he sailed.

He'd said as much once, to his grandmother. Nonna had rolled her eyes and reminded him that even though he towered over her now, that wouldn't stop her from whacking him across the backside if he needed it. A calm haven? Mama mia, what was he? A rowboat? Such a woman would bore him to tears in a month.

"A woman who can stand up to your Sicilian temper is what you need," Nonna had said.

Matthew grinned at the memory. His Nonna was right about most things, but she was wrong about this. Who knew what kind of woman he needed better than the man himself?

"And you're never going to meet the right woman if you don't look for her," Nonna had added, stamping her cane on the floor for good measure.

Well, he was looking. Slowly, maybe, but still, he was looking.

Matthew whistled as he strolled into the marble bathroom and turned on the shower.

Why rush something so pleasurable?

He shucked the boxer briefs he'd slept in, stepped into the stall, pressed his palms flat against the wall and bent his head. The water felt good, beating down on his neck and shoulders, and gave him time to think about the morning's agenda.

He smiled thinly. And what an agenda it was.

He was really looking forward to his meeting with the definitely snide and probably incompetent Susan Something-or-other. Madison? Washington? Coolidge? A President's name. Not that it mattered. Once it was on a severance check, Susan Whatever and her clever office memos would be history.

What sort of woman wrote stuff like that about a man she didn't even know? What sort of woman played games with one man and sent love and kisses to another?

A woman who thought the sexual revolution meant she could have the best of both worlds. Susan Hoover figured she could make the kinds of cracks about men that she'd undoubtedly condemned men for making about women, but she saw nothing wrong with insisting on gender neutrality when the situation suited her.

Matthew shut off the shower and reached for a towel. Oh, yeah. He had this broad figured out right down to the dotted line.

He strode into the bedroom and put on a pair of white briefs and navy socks. Then he opened the wall-to-wall mirrored closet and reached for a pale blue shirt.

The woman had made the most incredibly sexist comments about him, then done a one-eighty and blithely assumed she'd been passed over for promotion because she was female. And that was wrong. Dead wrong. Matthew had done a little research into *CHIC*. It had given him everything the company had about her, and from what he could see, Susan Whatever was about as qualified to head a magazine as she was to write material for a stand-up comic.

Which was why she had to go.

His eyes narrowed as he zipped the fly of his custom-tailored gray trousers and slipped on the matching jacket.

His decision had nothing to do with the stuff she'd said about him, that the women he dated were dumb or for calling him studly and brainless. Or for saying he figured he was the sexiest man alive.

He wasn't a vindictive man. It didn't mean a thing to him that half his team had read the woman's comments, that he'd heard the choked-back laughter at the next couple of meetings, that even now somebody on his staff would look at him and bite back a grin.

"It doesn't bother me in the slightest," Matthew said briskly to his reflection.

He snatched up his black leather briefcase, marched to the door, opened it and stepped into the hotel corridor.

"Damned right, it doesn't," he muttered, and slammed the door after him, so hard that it rattled.

CHAPTER TWO

IN HER college days, before Susannah had centered her studies on English lit, she'd taken a very popular philosophy course.

Professor Wheeler had made the round of all the talk shows with his theory of how to achieve happiness. Your successes and failures in life, he said, were dependent upon unwritten rules. Not the rules of physics, he'd add, with a condescending little smile, the ones that kept the earth from flying off into the sun or the polar ice caps from draining into the seas. The rules he referred to were very personal. Once you identified them, you could go through life secure in the knowledge that you had a Direction and a Purpose.

The best part was that you didn't have to wait, like Isaac Newton, and get conked on the head by an apple to discover them. Your Very Own Rules, according to Professor Wheeler, found you.

Six years had passed since then, and some of Susannah's personal rules had, indeed, discovered her. Unfortunately, as far as she could see, they had nothing to do with either Direction or Purpose—unless she planned to star in a low-budget sitcom.

Rule number one. White silk dresses worn to Italian restaurants meant the lasagna would fall into your lap. Rule number two. PMS was *not* an advertising gimmick dreamed up by Madison Avenue. Rule number three. Fat-free ice cream was.

Now, on a clear, chilly fall morning, she'd found not one more rule to add to her list but two.

Never trust an alarm clock on a day that could change your life.

Nobody but Superman could get from Greenwich Village to midtown Manhattan in less than twenty minutes during rush hour.

Sandwiched between an oversize woman who must have breakfasted on Garlic Krispies and a man who defended his eight inches of personal space with elbows that should have been classified as lethal weapons, Susannah rode the subway toward her destination.

Sardines had it better than this.

The train, packed with humanity, rumbled, rolled and rocked from side to side. Metal wheels screeched against the tracks. It was the ride from hell, but her fellow travelers, New York stoics all, showed no reaction. Susannah didn't, either. What was the point? She was trapped, she was late, she was going to make an entrance into the staff-filled boardroom with all the aplomb of a runaway train.

Susannah winced. Talk about bad images. Still, it was accurate. Why hadn't she planned the morning better? She should have set a backup alarm. She should have had extra shoelaces tucked away in the drawer. Forget the shoelaces. She had to set the standards now. She should have appeared at this meeting dressed in something that would have impressed everybody with her control and confidence.

If only she had a clever plan to toss on the table, maybe—just maybe—she could redeem herself. She'd spent the weekend on statistics. Why hadn't she spent it on ideas?

The train jolted to a halt. Susannah glanced out the window. The next station was hers. Her heart thumped. One more stop, then a four-block walk, and she'd be there.

"I need an idea," she whispered. "Just one idea."

"You need a head doctor," the fat woman said indignantly, through waves of garlic-scented breath.

Susannah nodded mournfully. "Maybe so," she said.

The train hurtled into the station. She fought her way to the door, across the platform and up the crowded stairs.

Out on the street, she began to run.

The taxi carrying Matthew Romano pulled to the curb outside the building that housed the *CHIC* offices.

Matthew paid the driver, collected his black leather briefcase from the seat beside him and stepped from the cab. A surprisingly cool wind sliced down the concrete canyon, and he turned up the collar of his raincoat as he took his first look at the *CHIC* building.

It was old, for New York. Matthew figured it dated back to the thirties, when Art Deco was all the rage. Grime coated the exterior and dulled the bronze doors, but he could still see the building's handsome lines beneath the dirt. He'd expected as much, considering that some of the brightest names in publishing had once been on the Elerbee Publications roster.

Matthew strode through the lobby to the elevators. He'd already decided to keep *CHIC*'s office space after he disposed of the magazine, but now he thought it might be worthwhile to check into the building itself. Elerbee owned it, didn't he?

Matthew reached into the inside breast pocket of his suit, took out a computerized recorder the size of a credit card and brought it to his lips.

"*CHIC* building," he said quietly. "Possible purchase?"

The elevator doors whisked open. Matthew put the recorder into his pocket and stepped into the car.

After this morning, *CHIC* was finished. His accountants would breathe a deep sigh of relief. Normally, he'd have put the magazine out of its misery as quickly and humanely as possible, but Susan Lincoln had made that impossible.

Not that he was vindictive, Matthew reminded himself as the elevator doors shut.

Not in the slightest.

Susannah came pounding around the corner.

The office was just ahead. She was in the home stretch. A minute to the lobby, another in the elevator…five minutes, max, she'd be at her desk. And then all she'd need was another few seconds to make a quick note about the absolutely incredible idea she'd come up with as she raced down the street from the subway.

She really had to start carrying a notebook. Or one of those little recorders.

But not today.

Susannah darted into the lobby and pounded the elevator

call button. Her reflection stared at her from the bronze doors, and she shuddered.

Lord, she was a mess!

The wind had not only dried her hair, it had churned it into what looked like finger-in-the-electric-outlet chic. There were two...three? Three buttons missing from the jacket she'd grabbed blindly on her way out the door. Her jeans...was that a paint smear from when she'd tried her hand at oils? And her sneakers... Susannah winced. Someplace between here and the subway, the safety pins had done a disappearing act. The sneaker had stayed on, though. All she had to do was remember not to make any quick moves with her right foot, and it would be fine.

She got into the elevator and punched the button for the fourteenth floor.

Okay. So she wasn't going to score points for haute couture. And she wasn't going to be on time or anywhere close to it. So what? It was silly to put too much emphasis on stuff like that. She had a new job title but she was still the same Susannah. She was, admittedly, just a tiny bit disorganized. But she was creative. Even old Elerbee, who'd hired and then promoted her, had understood that.

The staff knew her. She didn't have to impress anyone, she had to give them confidence and inspire them. And she was going to do exactly that with her fantastic new idea.

She could hardly wait to hear Claire's response, because this would be her baby. Claire was, after all, the new features editor.

The elevator doors slid open. Susannah stepped from the car.

Strange. The reception area was empty. Judy, the receptionist, was probably in the boardroom with the rest of the staff, but... Susannah smiled.

"Good girl," she murmured.

A fresh pot of coffee stood on a little sideboard, along with a platter heaped with doughnuts. Despite the hour, Judy had put out the refreshments that were a morning staple in reception.

Susannah hurried to her own office.

"Late, late, late," she whispered, glancing at the clock.

But not too late. It was almost eight twenty-five. All things considered, that wasn't too bad.

Quickly, she jotted some notes on a pad, grabbed her portable computer and her I Love Cape Cod souvenir mug and dashed to Judy's desk. Her stomach rumbled as she filled the mug to the brim. How did a person carry a pad, a computer, a mug filled with hot coffee and a doughnut without growing a third arm?

Susannah snagged a jelly doughnut, stuck it between her teeth, collected all her other paraphernalia and headed for the boardroom.

The door was closed.

That was unusual. The room wasn't all that big. Once everybody collected around the long cherry wood table, things generally seemed a bit crowded. It was better to leave the door open.

Never mind. Once they all heard her terrific idea for boosting *CHIC*'s sales and revamping its image, they'd be too busy smiling to worry about crowding.

Susannah hit the door with her elbow.

"Mmmf?" she said.

Nobody answered.

She gave it another try.

The door swung open.

They were all there, crammed even more closely together than usual, their eyes wide, their faces pale. Claire. Judy. Eddie, the mail-room intern. The fiction editor, the fashion gurus, the assistants and associates and staff photographers.

Everyone looked her up, then looked her down, but no one said a word, not even good morning.

At last, Claire stepped forward. "Suze," she whispered, and made a funny little motion with her head.

Did Claire have a crick in her neck? Susannah raised her eyebrows. "Mmmf?"

"Suze," Claire hissed.

"What Miss Haines is trying to say," a deep male voice said, "is that you're late, Miss Clinton."

Susannah stood absolutely still. She had never heard that voice before. She'd have remembered it if she had. Not many men could put a chill into the phrase, "You're late, Miss…"

Clinton? Who was Miss Clinton? And who was the man doing the talking?

Her gaze flew to Claire's. *Help me*, Susannah pleaded silently.

Claire grimaced, chewed on her lip, puffed out her breath, rolled her eyes. It was a performance that would have made Susannah giggle any other time. But now—now, Claire's strange mannerisms were an entire speech made without words.

The implication, though, was absolutely clear.

Warning! Claire was saying, *warning!* Whoever the man was, he was trouble with a capital T. But Susannah had already figured that out. Who else could enter the *CHIC* offices and position himself at the head of the conference table in the boardroom but a man who was trouble?

But who was he? Who could he be?

Someone from Update. There was no other possibility.

Susannah swallowed dryly. Of course! This was the bean counter she'd been expecting, the one she'd known would march in, demand access to all *CHIC*'s records, intimidate the staff and then, a few days later, take off his bifocals, clean them with the tip of his tie while he informed her that he was going to recommend that *CHIC* be shut down.

But the voice at the head of the table didn't sound as if it went with a skinny little man who wore bifocals.

"Well, Miss Clinton? I'm waiting to hear your excuse for your lateness." The deep voice took on a silken purr. Susannah had a sudden mental image of a big cat—a puma, maybe, or a jaguar—wearing a pair of horn-rimmed glasses. "We're all waiting, Miss Clinton. Won't you enlighten us? Tell us why you called your staff in for a meeting to be held promptly at eight o'clock when you yourself didn't think it important enough to appear until—" there was a brief pause, as if the cat were peering through its horn-rims at its watch "—until twenty minutes of nine?"

Susannah threw one last, desperate look in Claire's direction.

"Mmmf?" she breathed, past the doughnut, the damned stupid doughnut, still clutched between her teeth.

Claire gave her a wan smile, lifted a hand and made a slicing motion across her throat.

Oh, God, Susannah thought, as everybody stepped back, parting like the Red Sea so the conference table, all twelve feet of it, came into view.

And so did the man seated at its head.

No, Susannah thought dizzily. He wasn't a jaguar. He wasn't a puma. He was a hawk. A magnificent hawk, with the fierce look of the predator in his eyes. And those eyes... Her stomach clenched.

Those blue, blue eyes were fixed coldly on her.

She felt her knees wobble. This was no skinny, middle-aged bean counter with bifocals. This was not the man from Update. This was—

"Good morning, Miss Clinton," Matthew Romano said.

Susannah's mouth dropped open. The doughnut left a snowfall of sugar across Beethoven's face as it tumbled to the shiny tile floor. Bright red jelly oozed across the toe of the sneaker that had been held together by safety pins.

Romano smiled.

"Charming," he said, almost purring, as his gaze swept over her. "Is this a new style, or what?"

A muffled sound, half laugh, half groan, broke the silence. Susannah glared at Claire, who clapped her hand over her mouth and shook her head in mute apology.

"Nothing to say?" His smile tilted, became as icy as his eyes. "What a pity, Miss Clinton. I didn't expect you'd ever find yourself at a loss for words, particularly where I'm concerned."

Susannah's stricken gaze followed him as he rose lazily to his feet.

He looked as if he'd just stepped from the pages of *Gentleman's Quarterly.* The dark, expertly cut hair. The hard, handsome face. The perfectly tailored suit, pale blue shirt and elegantly knotted tie. She couldn't see his shoes, but she knew they'd be as polished as mirrors.

Quickly, she shifted her weight, trying to hide the jelly-covered toe of the laceless sneaker.

Romano folded his arms and laughed.

Color flew into Susannah's face. What was Romano doing

here? Why was he trying to humiliate her? Well, he wouldn't succeed. She'd act like a lady, even though it was obvious that he was no gentleman.

"How nice to meet you, Mr. Romano. Perhaps you'd be kind enough to explain your presence here."

Matthew arched one eyebrow. For a woman who looked as if she were dressed for the rag pickers ball, a woman who surely hadn't expected to find him camped on *CHIC*'s doorstep, so to speak, Susan Whatever was certainly managing to seem cool and collected.

She wasn't, of course. He could see it in the bright flush in her cheeks and in the almost imperceptible tremor that had gone through her body when she'd first seen him sitting at the conference table.

His gaze drifted over her again. *This* was the editor-in-chief of the magazine? The person Elerbee had entrusted with the formidable job of turning *CHIC* into a money-making property? The old man must have gone soft in the head. Nothing else could explain it. Susan...Clinton? Truman? The woman looked as if she'd picked her clothes out of a bin at the nearest Goodwill, styled her hair by sticking a finger into an electrical outlet, and her sneakers...

Unless he was losing his mind, the one that had jelly on it had no laces.

"You *are* Matthew Romano, aren't you?"

Matthew's gaze met hers. She'd had time to gather herself, he could see. The hot color had left her face. She was, in fact, pale—except for her eyes. They were so bright they looked almost feverish. Were they hazel? Green? Actually, he'd never seen a color quite like them, almost golden, but flecked with chips of jade and tourmaline.

"Claire?"

Susannah spoke without looking away from Romano. Her heart was banging in her chest, but her voice was clipped. Claire's, on the other hand, was a paper-thin whisper.

"Y-yes?"

"Call security."

"What?"

"You heard me. Call security. Tell them we have an intruder."

"Susannah." Claire moved quickly to her friend's side. "Suze, listen—"

"If you won't do it," Susannah said, her eyes never leaving Romano's face, "I will. Hand me the phone."

"Oh, Suze. Suze, you've got to lis—"

Susannah snatched up the telephone. "Last chance, Mr. Romano. Either you explain your unwanted, uninvited presence in these offices, or I'll have you thrown out. Do I make myself clear?"

"Perfectly."

"Well?"

He smiled, stepped from behind the table and leaned a hip against the wall. She'd been right, she thought, dazed. You could probably use his shoes for mirrors.

"I own them."

Susannah blinked. "I beg your pardon?"

"These offices. This room." He lifted his hand and waved it nonchalantly through the air. "I own it all, Miss Clinton."

"My name is— Own it how? Mr. Elerbee sold out to Update Publications."

"Yes, that's right. And I am Update." He grinned, and she could see he was enjoying this. "What's the matter, Miss Clinton? Don't you like surprises?"

Susannah felt as if the air were being sucked from her lungs.

Matthew Romano had bought *CHIC*. He, not some faceless group of stockholders, was Update Publications.

This was it, then.

So much for all the time she'd spent worrying about how to resurrect *CHIC* magazine. For all the sleepless nights and late meetings. So much for her job, for her chance to prove herself. So much for *all* their jobs, every last one of them.

CHIC was finished. The news was written all over Romano's face, etched in his arrogant, I-am-God smile. He'd come here to plunge a dagger into the magazine's barely beating heart, though why he'd wanted to do it himself was anybody's guess.

I didn't expect you'd ever find yourself at a loss for words, particularly where I'm concerned.

The words he'd spoken a few minutes ago seemed to ring

in her ears. Susannah stared at him. He'd come to do the job himself as a way of getting even with her. This was personal. A vendetta involving Romano and her. But he was going to take his revenge on everybody who worked here.

"No comment, Miss Clinton? That's too bad. I was sure you'd have something interesting to say."

Behind her, someone tittered nervously. Romano didn't so much as smile.

"I'm pleased to see you recognize me. I was concerned that you wouldn't be able to do so without me having a blonde on my arm. I thought about renting one for the occasion, but it seems blondes—even dumb ones—aren't available so early in the day."

Another giggle rose in the crowd. Matthew's eyes flashed. He jerked his head toward the door.

"You're free to leave," he said. "All of you."

It was a command, not an offer, and nobody was foolish enough to ignore it. People scuttled for the exit. Even Claire, Susannah noted with horror. Not that she could blame her. Claire wanted to hang onto her job. They all did. But Romano had no intention of leaving them with jobs to hang onto. Soon enough, they'd all know that.

He waited until the room was empty. Then he strolled past Susannah and shut the door with a gentleness that made her flinch.

"Now," he said pleasantly, "let's get down to business."

Susannah turned and looked at him. Business? What kind of business? Romano lounged against the closed door, hands tucked casually into his pockets, but the pose, she knew, was deceptive. Anger emanated from him like some hot, primal male hormone.

Her mouth went dry.

Close up, Matthew Romano was intimidating. It wasn't just his height, though he towered over her. It wasn't just his build, though not even the quietly expensive suit could hide all the muscle. It was the way he held himself, the look in his eyes, the cool little smile that curled his lips. It was everything that made him what he was, who he was.

"Does the mention of business always make you go pale, Miss Clinton?"

Apparently, he'd read her mail. Weren't there privacy laws against that kind of thing?

"Spying is what makes me go pale, Mr. Romano." Her voice was cool and steady. There was, she told herself, no way he could know that a psychotic drummer seemed to have taken up residence behind her ribs.

"Spying, Miss Clinton?"

"Spying. Prying. Poking into someone's private correspondence. Don't look so surprised, Mr. Romano. It's quite obvious that's what you've done. You've read my mail, and you had no right to do that."

"I'm sorry to disillusion you, Miss Clinton, but what you write on company memos, on company stationery, on the company's E-mail account, is not yours. It's mine."

"That's ridiculous!"

"Tell that to the courts. They decided the issue years ago." Romano's eyes flashed. "Your tasteless mental meanderings have had quite a large readership."

Oh, God. Was he right? Her brain whirled. What, exactly, had she written? Nothing complimentary. But how bad could it have been?

Very bad, she thought, as bits and pieces came back to her. Very, very bad.

"Remarkable, isn't it?" His smile was bright, almost cheery. "You know so much about me. And you didn't hesitate to comment on what you knew. My taste in women. My unfortunate lack of intellect. My conviction that I'm sexy." He smiled. "Even what I'd look like as a centerfold."

Please, Susannah thought, *Oh, please, please let the floor open up beneath me.*

His smile still glittered, but there was a sudden darkness in his eyes that made her breath hitch.

"And my—how did you put it? Ah, yes. My 'studliness.'"

Susannah's cheeks flamed.

"I don't supposed you'd care to define that word."

"I didn't mean... I never meant to imply..."

He took a step forward. She took a quick step back. Her foot slipped out of the laceless sneaker, but there was no time to stop and recover it, there was only time to step back again, because he was still coming.

"Oh, but you did," he said softly. "You meant every word of it, and that's really remarkable, considering that we've never met until this morning. I'm right, aren't I, Miss Clinton?"

She shook her head. She nodded. Speech was out of the question.

"What was that?" His smile grew even brighter. "That shake of the head. A denial that you meant what you wrote? An admittance that we never met before?"

"No," Susannah whispered miserably. "I mean, we've never—"

"Ah." He nodded. "But you determined my studliness nonetheless, is that right?"

"Mr. Romano." She licked her lips. "I may have been a little out of line, but—"

"A little?" He closed the distance remaining between them and looked coldly at her as her shoulders hit the wall. "Fascinating, Miss Clinton, how cautious your use of the language has suddenly become. For a woman given to such interesting hyperbole, I mean." His eyes, dark and deep, fastened on hers. "Once again, I'm asking you to tell me what you mean by that word."

Susannah swallowed hard. He was close. Too close. She could smell the faint scent of soap on his skin, see the shadow of stubble on his jaw and chin. His lashes were dark and thick. His nose was perfectly straight except for a barely perceptible tilt midway down its length.

He looked cold and hard and angry.

And studly.

He was studly, indeed, she thought dizzily. Her heart did what felt like a somersault in her chest. If you liked the type.

She didn't.

"Well?" He smiled slyly, slapped a hand on either side of the wall beside her and lowered his head. "I'm waiting, Miss Clinton."

Their eyes met. The moment held, then lengthened.

"Mr. Romano," Susannah whispered. "Mr. Romano, please…"

Mr. Romano, please?

What in hell was happening here? The man had come strutting into her office—and it *was* hers, until he fired her—to humiliate her. And she, like an idiot, was letting him get away with it.

Susannah lifted her chin.

"Actually," she said, "I should thank you."

It was his turn to blink. She almost laughed at the sight.

"Thank me?" he asked cautiously, and she nodded.

"For this demonstration." He drew back, frowning. Susannah saw her chance and took it, ducking out from under his arm, smiling coolly as she danced away. "In fact, since— as you pointed out—I made a few public comments about you, I'll be happy to also make a public retraction."

"A retraction?"

She nodded. She had him now. Oh, the confused look on his handsome—if you liked the type—face! "It will be my pleasure to tell the world that I was wrong. You are most definitely not studly." She eyed him up and down. "I don't think you could turn a real woman on if you tried."

His face went white, and something that sounded suspiciously like a growl broke from his throat. Warning sirens shrieked in Susannah's head, but she wasn't about to stop.

"But I'll stand behind everything else I said about you. You're an arrogant SOB, and now that we've met, I understand your propensity for blondes. Dumb ones, I mean. Let's face it, Mr. Romano. They're the only ones who'd put up with your overinflated ego."

That last sound had definitely been a growl. He was moving, heading toward her, with a glint in his eye that was truly terrifying.

Susannah picked up speed. It wasn't easy, making for the door while going backward, especially since she'd left one sneaker behind, but she kept going until she figured she had only to reach back to touch the doorknob.

"As for this job, and your magazine, you know what you can do with them, Mr. Romano. Oh, by the way, my surname isn't Clinton. It's Madison, as in James Madison, the fourth president of the United States—if that's not too much for you to remember. When you write out my severance check, please make it out properly, to Madison. Susannah Madison. Capital M, a, d, i, s, o, n."

She laughed. She couldn't help it. Studliness had given way to fury, and the sight warmed her heart.

"Goodbye, Mr. Romano. Have a nice— Whoa!''

Susannah's bare foot went down on something soft and slippery. In the blink of an eye, she was airborne.

CHAPTER THREE

IT ALL seemed to happen in slow motion.

The woman with one sneaker. The jelly doughnut on the floor—

The pratfall.

Matthew leaped into action, coming up behind her, catching her in midair before she could hit the floor.

There hadn't seemed to be much to her, as far as he'd been able to see. She was small and skinny, not curvy the way a woman ought to be. But she was a full armload. Her weight, as she fell against him, had enough force to knock the breath out of them both.

"Ooof," he gasped, as his arms closed around her.

He lurched, staggered, tripped over his own feet. Susannah gave a thin shriek. She turned, and her arms closed around his neck, and whatever air he might have drawn in to replace what he'd exhaled never made it to his lungs.

What could a man who is being choked to death say to the woman who was choking him?

"Aagh," Matthew said, backpedaling wildly.

Overbalancing, they skated in reverse, smashed into the table, careened off a cabinet and fell into the unforgiving embrace of the high-backed armchair Matthew had been sitting in before Susannah Madison had come marching through the door.

The chair groaned, flew backward and glanced off the table. A lamp went down with a crash, followed by the telephone, which made a sad, tinkling sound as it hit the floor.

And then, mercifully, there was silence.

But just for a second.

Somebody pounded on the closed boardroom door.

"Suze?" Claire's voice was shrill. "Suze, are you okay?"

Matthew dragged one of Susannah's arms from around his neck.

"She's fine," he called.

Susannah glared at him. "I'm not—"

He clamped a hand over her mouth.

"You want them to see this mess?" he hissed, his mouth at her ear. "Do you have an explanation that's going to keep everybody out there from figuring we just slugged it out?"

Susannah threw a wild look around the room. Papers were strewn across the floor. The heavy conference table stood at an angle to the wall. The lamp had shattered, and the telephone was emitting a pathetic bleep. And on top of all that, here she was, sitting cozily in Matthew Romano's lap.

She wrapped her hand around his and lifted it from her mouth.

"Everything's fine, Claire," she called. "Just fine."

"You sure?"

"Positive." Positive? The room looked as if an inmate had rearranged the furniture in the asylum. For a second, Susannah wanted to burst out laughing.

"Mr. Romano, ah, Mr. Romano had a little accident, that's all."

"Mr. Romano had an accident?" Matthew whispered indignantly.

A tremor raced along her skin as his breath tickled her ear.

"He, um, he backed into the table. And, uh, some stuff fell down."

There was silence. Susannah could imagine the way Claire and the rest would be looking at each other.

"Okay," Claire said finally, "but if you want me, I'll be right in my office."

Susannah nodded. "Yeah," she muttered, "great."

Footsteps tapped down the hall. She waited a moment and then cleared her throat.

"You can let me up now, Mr. Romano."

"Are you sure you're okay?"

"I'm fine."

"What's with the martyred tone of voice, Madison? This mess wasn't my idea, you know."

"Well, it certainly wasn't mine!"

"No. That's true enough. Attempting a crash landing on your butt was definitely your idea."

Susannah glared at Matthew, and he glared back. Oh, hell, she thought. He was right. If he hadn't managed to grab her, to break her fall...

"I suppose there's some validity to that," she said stiffly.

"Is that supposed to be a thank-you?"

Susannah blew out a breath. A dark curl lifted on her forehead.

"Very well. Thank you."

Matthew grinned. She'd said the words as if he were an executioner who'd just offered to cut off her head with a newly sharpened blade instead of a dull one.

"You see? It didn't hurt, did it?"

"Don't push it, Mr. Romano," she said, fixing him with a cold eye. "You got your thank-you. Leave it at that. I don't suppose you'd believe I'm not usually so clumsy."

"Actually, Miss Madison, you stepped on something."

Susannah shifted her weight and looked at him. Not a good idea, Matthew thought. Shifting like that, while she was sitting in his lap. Whatever had made him think she was skinny? She wasn't an armful, he had to admit, but skinny? Not with those firm breasts brushing against his chest. Not with that nicely rounded little bottom against his thighs.

"Stepped on what?" she said.

Matthew frowned, cleared his throat and dragged his mind back to the conversation.

"A jelly doughnut."

Susannah's brows shot skyward. "A jelly—" Delicate waves of pink surged into her cheeks. "Oh, damn."

"Yup. You might say that you really put your foot into it this time."

He knew the image would be forever etched into his memory. Susannah, figuring she'd leveled him with a barrage of words, making for the door with a clever exit in mind until one sneakerless foot came down on the doughnut and she executed a takeoff that could have only been improved by a guy with a big red nose and a clown suit.

Matthew couldn't help it. He snorted. Big mistake. He knew it instantly, but it was too late.

Susannah's eyes flashed.

"You find this amusing, Mr. Romano?"

"No," he said, shaking his head, "no, certainly not. It's just…"

Oh, hell. He couldn't help it. He snorted again.

Her face flamed. "I was right," she said, slamming her hand against his chest. "You really are a horrible human being! I almost broke my neck, and you sit there laughing?"

"I'm not. Laughing at you, I mean. It's just that—"

"It was all your fault, anyway. I'd never have slipped if you hadn't come after me."

"Now, wait just a minute, Miss Madison. I did not—"

"You did. I should have expected it. I mean, a man like you would never let anybody get away with one-upping him."

Matthew jerked back. "What are you talking about?"

"You know what I'm talking about," Susannah said coldly. "I showed you up for the rat you are, and you couldn't handle it. So you—you came stalking after me."

"I what?"

"Who knew what you were going to do? No wonder I tried to get away. No wonder I tripped and fell. No wonder—"

"Either you're a world-class liar, Miss Madison—"

"I never lie, Mr. Romano!"

"Or you've got an imagination big enough to fill this room!"

"Are you trying to deny that you came after me a few minutes ago?"

Matthew glared at her. "Are you trying to deny that you insulted me?"

"I just told you the truth."

"You insulted me, Miss Madison. And you challenged my manhood."

Susannah blinked. "Excuse me?"

"All that garbage about me not being able to turn a real woman on and dumb blondes being the only ones who'd go out with me—"

"Not all blondes are dumb, of course," she said, smiling sweetly. "I guess that limits your field."

Matthew's eyes narrowed. "Doesn't it bother you to condemn the members of your own sex that way?"

"Why should it? I'm not a card-carrying feminist. I believe in equal opportunity for women, but I don't believe all women are equal. If there are lowbrow idiots out there who can be turned on by a man with a lot of money and a little bit of looks—a very little bit—so be it.''

"So, I'm incapable of turning a woman on?"

"If she doesn't owe points on an intelligence scale? Damned right, Mr. Romano!''

"Would it surprise you to know that the woman I'm currently seeing is an attorney?"

Susannah laughed. Dammit, he didn't blame her. What was he going to do? Trot out the pedigree of every female in his past?

"I suppose," he said coldly, "your IQ is high enough so that you consider yourself immune to—how did you put it? A man with a whole lot of money and a little bit of good looks.''

"Definitely."

"That, then, is why you don't find me..." He smiled nastily. "What was your phrase, Miss Madison? Ah, yes. Studly.''

Pink color swept into her cheeks. What kind of conversation was this? And why were they having it with her seated in Matthew Romano's lap?

In his lap? Good grief! What she doing still sitting, in his arms?

Susannah pulled back.

"Let me up, please."

"Does Peter have a whole lot of money and a little bit of good looks?"

"What?"

What, indeed? Why had he asked her about Peter? The men in Susannah Madison's life were none of his business.

"What do you know about Peter?" she demanded. "Have you been spying on my private life, too?"

"The next time you send hugs and kisses to the man in your life, don't do it via office E-mail."

"That's it," Susannah said with quiet fury. "Let me up,!"

It was, Matthew knew, a logical request. There was no reason to keep her here, with her spiky hair inches from his nose. He leaned closer and sniffed. Her hair smelled faintly of flowers. And it only looked spiky. When his nose brushed against it, it felt silky. And soft.

"If you don't let me up, I'll—"

"You'll what?" He chuckled. "Yell? Scream? Call for your colleagues to break down the door and see their boss cozily occupying the lap of the studly enemy?"

Lord, oh, lord, why had she ever called him that?

"I am not cozily occupying your lap," she said, with great dignity. "And I've already told you, you are not—"

"Studly?" Matthew said, and laughed.

The laugh, sly and low in his throat, did it. Susannah punched her fist into his shoulder.

"Let go," she said furiously. "And tell me what's so damned funny!"

"You, Miss Madison. You seem to think you can waltz through life saying whatever you like about people without ever having to pay the price."

"If you mean that I speak my mind—"

"I mean exactly what I said. You've made some unpleasant accusations about me."

"Let go," Susannah panted, as she struggled to free herself from his arms.

Romano held her tighter.

"Unpleasant, and unwarranted. And I resent it."

"Too bad."

Matthew shifted his weight in the chair. The sudden movement tipped Susannah forward. Without thinking, she threw both arms around his neck to recapture her balance.

"Do you happen to know your IQ, Miss Madison?"

Susannah looked at Matthew Romano. His face was inches from hers, the cool blue eyes bottomless. She could see a tiny scar feathering out from beneath one eyebrow. Did it have something to do with that little jog in his nose? Somehow or other, despite the expensive suit, the faint but elegant cologne, the trappings of wealth that clung to this man, she had no difficulty picturing him getting his nose broken or his forehead cut. There was something intensely masculine about Matthew Romano, something that could surely make female hearts flutter.

Close up, he wasn't quite the empty suit she'd imagined.

Actually, there was nothing empty about this suit, nothing at all. The arms that held her were powerful. The chest she leaned against was muscular, as were the thighs that cradled her bottom.

Susannah flushed.

All right. Perhaps there were things about him some women might find attractive. Some. Not her.

"Doing an assessment?" he asked softly.

Susannah blinked. "I beg your pardon?"

Matthew's smile tilted. "You seemed to be taking inventory, Miss Madison. I wonder—do I come up to par?"

"I don't know what you're talking about," she said coldly.

He laughed, and settled his arms more comfortably around her. "Let's return to my question, shall we? Do you know your IQ?"

"I don't see what my IQ has to do with anything, Mr. Romano."

"Humor me."

Susannah folded her arms. "Take two of your female friends, add them together and tack on half of one more, and you're getting close."

Matthew grinned. "That's perfect."

"I've always thought so."

"It's excellent."

"I'm delighted you approve, but I fail to see what my IQ has to do with anything."

"It's quite simple, Miss Madison." Matthew shifted her so that she was facing him. "I'm going to prove that you're wrong, and I want to be sure to do it by a wide enough margin."

"What?" Susannah said.

It was all she had time to say, because less than a heartbeat later, Matthew Romano's mouth closed over hers.

His lips were firm and warm. They settled over hers with an authority that, for a second, anyway, stunned her into immobility.

But it didn't last.

He knew the instant reality hit. She went from shocked compliance to horrified rigidity in his arms. Next, she'd begin to struggle. Except he wouldn't let things go that far.

Matthew wasn't a man who got pleasure from overpowering women. Pleasure, especially sexual pleasure, came from giving as well as receiving. He liked to feel a woman's heartbeat quicken, to have her sigh his name and turn to warm honey in his arms. And he certainly didn't enjoy making love to a woman he found unattractive, in spirit as well as body.

As soon as Susannah Madison began fighting him, he would let her go. All this was about, all he wanted, was to show her for the sharp-tongued witch she was.

She couldn't claw his male dignity to shreds and get away with it.

It was a fine idea. Unfortunately, there were factors he'd failed to take into consideration.

The softness of Susannah's mouth.

The scent of her skin.

The race of her heart.

The feel of her in his arms.

He'd expected to be kissing a sour old maid. But he found himself kissing a dream instead.

She began to struggle. It was time to let her go.

But he didn't want to.

He wanted to stroke her hair. To slip his tongue into her mouth. To shape her body with his hands and taste all its sweet, hidden places.

"Susannah," he whispered against her lips. "Susannah."

He sank his hands into her hair, fit his mouth more carefully over hers and softened the kiss. And all at once she wasn't fighting him. She was kissing him back.

She was kissing him, this man who'd just forced his kiss upon her, this man she'd despised on sight. She was kissing him, and loving it.

The taste of him.

The feel.

The incredible hardness of his body.

The shocking tenderness of his mouth.

What am I doing? Susannah asked herself. And then she gave up thinking and tumbled into the magic of the kiss.

She'd never known a kiss could be like this, that her heart could hammer in her throat just at the feel of a man's lips on hers. The sensation was beyond comprehension. She felt as if she were slipping away from herself, and it was wonderful. Nothing existed but the moment and Matthew.

He moved so that she was lying fully against him. When he did, she lifted her arms and wound them around his neck. There was a thudding sound somewhere in the distance. Was it the sound of her heart?

Was somebody calling her name?

Was a voice saying, "Suze?"

It wasn't Matthew. He hadn't seemed to know her name a little while ago. Now he was holding her, kissing her, whispering "Susannah," over and over against her lips.

"Matthew," she sighed.

He groaned, bent his head, gently nipped her throat.

She dug her fingers into his hair. Desire shot through her. She felt reckless and bold.

He was silk and steel, fire and ice. And she was burning.

His hand swept up, cupped her breast. She arched against the caress, riding the sensation of his touch. Her breath caught in an ecstatic sob as he shoved up her sweatshirt and stroked his fingertips over the satin of her flesh. She cried out and ground her bottom against the hardness of him.

He rose, holding her. His embrace was powerful. She felt fragile, eager, filled with need for him. She clung to him, her hands locked behind his head, her mouth opening to his hot, hungry kisses. Papers, books, pencils flew from the conference table as he lay her down upon it.

"Susannah," he said fiercely.

She looked at him. His eyes were hot and dark with desire.

A shudder raced through her. She knew that what was going to happen between them would change her life forever, would make any other lover impossible.

"Yes," she said, raising her arms to him, "yes, yes..."

The door swung open, hitting the wall like a clap of thunder rolling over the canyons of the city. "Oh, my God! Susannah!"

Susannah almost fell off the table.

She sat up. Matthew stepped back. Both of them stared at the open door, where Claire and Eddie and Judy and, Susannah thought desperately, what looked like a million other *CHIC* staffers stood crowded together in stunned silence. It was like staring into a sea of disbelief. Mouths hung open. Eyes grew round as saucers. Heads swiveled, as if this were a tennis match, while everyone looked from Susannah to Matthew, from Matthew to Susannah...

Susannah's stomach clenched as the enormity of what had happened—what had almost happened—began seeping in. She'd almost—she and Matthew Romano had almost—they had come very close to—

And, as if that weren't awful enough, everybody at *CHIC* knew it. And she would have to live with that forever.

"Suze?"

Susannah shut her eyes, then blinked them open. Claire was staring at her as if she were a stranger. Why wouldn't she? She knew how she must look. Her disheveled clothes. Her hot face. Her kiss-swollen lips.

"Claire," she said. Her voice sounded rusty, and she cleared her throat and began again. "I know how this must look, but—"

But? But what? *But the man standing beside me, the one I swear to you I absolutely, positively, wholeheartedly abhor, hate and despise, kissed me, simply kissed me, and I went crazy?*

"Claire." Susannah lifted her hands in a gesture of defeat. "I know what you want to hear. But—but really, I can't—I just can't explain why—why—"

"Of course she can't," Matthew Romano said.

Authority resonated in his deep voice. Every eye swiveled in his direction, Susannah's included. He looked perfectly at ease and in control of the situation. Not even his tie was askew.

"Can't what?" Claire asked suspiciously.

Good question, Susannah thought, and waited for the detestable Mr. Romano to field it. He did, along with a smile that oozed concern.

"She can't explain why she fainted, Miss...?"

"Haines," Claire said, and looked even more suspiciously at Susannah. "You fainted?"

Susannah licked her lips. "Ah... Yes. Yes, that's right. I fainted."

Claire's brow furrowed. "Why?"

"Why?" Susannah asked stupidly, and Claire nodded.

"That's what I said, Suze. Why'd you faint? People don't simply keel over for no reason at all."

Susannah looked at Matthew. *You're the one with the answers,* her eyes said, *so go ahead. Come up with a good one.*

"It was the shock," Romano said smoothly, and offered her his hand. "Miss Madison? Are you feeling well enough to stand?"

"Thank you." Her tone was as polite as his. "I don't need any help."

But she did. Her legs weren't as steady as her voice. She rocked on her heels when she slid from the table, and he slipped a gentlemanly arm around her shoulders.

"Easy does it, Miss Madison. You don't want to push yourself, considering the shock you just had."

"What shock?" Claire asked. Her gaze narrowed, focused on Matthew's face and then on Susannah's. "Suze? Answer me."

Susannah patted down her hair, smoothed down her sweatshirt, avoided looking at her jelly-smeared foot and spoke as demurely as if she were still in Miss Porter's seventh-grade dance class.

"I would, but I'm sure Mr. Romano can explain it better than I can."

Matthew smiled. It was that same insolent smile she'd disliked from the first, and it galled her to think he could manage it, even now.

"Why, the shock of hearing that I've decided to give all of you four weeks to try to turn *CHIC* around."

There was a second of dumbstruck silence, and then somebody gave a whoop of delight. It was just enough to muffle Susannah's stunned whisper.

"What?" she asked. "What?"

Matthew's arm tightened around her shoulders. "Surprised?" he asked softly.

Susannah nodded. She stared at him, and slowly a little smile tugged at the corners of her mouth. Maybe she'd misjudged him. Maybe he wasn't such a rat, after all. Maybe...

"That's great!" Claire was almost dancing with excitement. "We all thought—well, considering how things were going between you and Suze, we figured..."

"I've had a change of heart, " Matthew said, "and you owe it all to Miss Madison."

A warning buzz sounded in Susannah's ears.

"It wasn't me," she said quickly. "I didn't do anything."

"Come now, Miss Madison." Matthew was almost purring. "Don't be so modest."

"Yeah, Suze." Eddie grinned from ear to ear. "What'd she do to win you over, Mr. Romano? Quote you facts and figures? Dream up some new ad campaign?" He chuckled. "Suze can be real persuasive when she puts her mind to it."

"Oh, she certainly can."

Matthew's smile made her heart stop.

"I didn't," she said. "I mean, I never suggested—"

"Of course she did," he said gently, though his fingers were biting hard into her flesh. "Miss Madison spent the last few minutes doing her best to persuade me that she has the talent to make me a very happy man."

Panic beat through Susannah's blood. "No! No, I did no such—"

"Don't be modest, Suze." Claire grinned at Matthew. "And she succeeded, huh?"

"Oh, yes," he said softly, his eyes locked on Susannah's. "Luckily for you all, she most certainly did."

"Way to go, Suze," Eddie cried.

The little crowd began to cheer.

"Bastard," Susannah whispered, but nobody but Matthew could hear her, and he just laughed, chucked her under the chin, saluted his fans and strolled from the room.

CHAPTER FOUR

MATTHEW whistled softly through his teeth as he rode the elevator to the lobby.

Damn, but this had been a good morning's work.

He'd come here to deal with Susannah Madison. And, by God, deal with her he had. Oh, if only he'd had a camera to record the look on her face when she came sauntering through the door of the boardroom and laid eyes on him!

Matthew chuckled and leaned against the wall, hands tucked in his pockets. It was a moment he'd never forget. Her shock. Her disbelief. The dismay that had glinted in those brown eyes.

Hazel eyes. Her eyes were hazel.

He frowned, took his hands from his pockets and folded his arms.

Who gave a damn what color her eyes were?

Maybe they were green. Yes, green was more like it, and shot with flecks of gold.

Matthew's frown deepened. He stepped away from the wall of the elevator and jabbed the button for the lobby floor in frustration.

"Come on," he muttered, and shot an impatient glance at the indicator panel above the door. Twelve. Eleven. Ten. How long could it take to go fourteen floors?

As for Madison's eyes, what did the color matter? He'd evened the score, hadn't he? That was what counted. By moving quickly, he'd caught Susannah Madison unexpectedly. With her pants down, so to speak.

Oh, hell.

He scrubbed a hand across his face.

What an image *that* was!

The last thing he wanted to think about was Susannah Madison with her pants down, she of the topaz eyes—because that was what they were. She had topaz eyes, a soft mouth, skin that had turned hot and silken at his touch...

Matthew's anatomy responded to the unplanned inventory with breathtaking speed.

"Damnation!"

He slammed the lobby button again, which was obviously a mistake, because the car shuddered, groaned and came to a dead stop. The doors didn't move. He looked at the old-fashioned indicator panel. The arrow sat neatly between numbers eight and nine.

"Great," Matthew snarled. "Just great."

He punched the emergency button, waited for the sound of the alarm bell...and heard only silence. He hit the button again, and the car gave a jolt. Slowly, at a rate of what seemed an inch an hour, it began its descent.

Matthew cursed, leaned against the wall, folded his arms and settled in to wait.

First the incident in the boardroom, now a cranky elevator. This was turning out to be one great day.

Where had he left his brain this morning? It wasn't between his ears. There was no other way to explain why he'd given up rational thought as soon as the Madison woman had come sashaying into view with her laceless sneaker, her hairstyle-by-electric-outlet. And that doughnut between her teeth.

Oh, yeah. Without question, wasn't that a description sexy enough to put any red-blooded American male's gonads into overdrive?

Matthew glared at his reflection in the smudged brass elevator door.

"You're behaving like an idiot, Romano," he muttered.

His reflection knew better than to argue. Besides, it was true.

It was bad enough he'd succumbed to an emotion as petty as revenge and had flown three thousand miles across the country to get it. Revenge, and never mind all his speeches about not being a vindictive man. He'd let the sophomoric remarks of a woman he'd never met tick him off.

And he'd ended up making an ass of himself.

Why had he kissed Susannah Madison?

Kissed her? *Kissed her?* Matthew rolled his eyes. If that was just a kiss, he'd left Planet Earth behind.

What he'd done was damn near jump her bones. Ten minutes after he'd met her. In the boardroom. On the conference table. With a crowd of thousands in the hall.

Matthew's shoulders slumped.

Was he nuts, or was he nuts? What had happened to his control over the situation, over Susannah Madison...over himself?

It wasn't even as if she'd turned him on. The thought was almost enough to make him laugh. Turned on by a woman with a razor-sharp tongue and the charm of a rattlesnake? Turned on by somebody who looked like a refugee from a sideshow?

The sweatshirt. The jeans. The sneakers. Oh, yes, the sneakers.

He did laugh, this time.

A bag lady had more going for her than the Madison broad...and yet, if the *CHIC* staffers hadn't come bursting through the door, he'd have—she'd have—they'd have...

"Damnation," Matthew said again, and wiped his hand over his suddenly sweaty brow.

Was he losing his taste? His touch? His mind?

What in hell would make a man hit on a woman who didn't even look like a woman? Well, okay. She'd looked like a woman. There'd been the curve of her breasts, even under the baggy shirt. The feel of that nice, rounded bottom beneath the saggy jeans. The smell of her hair, the length of her lashes, the pouty mouth.

There had to be an explanation for his behavior. Anger? Could that have been the reason? Could his rage at Susannah Madison have somehow translated itself into desire?

No way.

Sex was sex. Rage was rage. Only a complete idiot would confuse the two.

"Do I really look like an idiot?" Matthew demanded of his reflection just as the doors swooshed open on the lobby.

A small, stout woman, arms crammed with file folders, eyed him warily. Matthew felt a strange sensation begin crawling up his neck. He was blushing! Blushing, and all because a broad who'd already maligned him on paper had managed to humiliate him in person.

"No." The woman's voice quavered. "You, ah, you look like a perfectly normal human being to me."

Matthew felt the heat rise into his face. "I wasn't talking to you," he said stiffly.

"Sure. Whatever you say, mister. There's no need to explain, no need at—"

Matthew started past her, stopped and swung around.

"Would you answer a question, please, madam?"

I already did," the woman said quickly. "You said—"

"Forget that," he said, with a dismissive wave of the hand. "I was talking to myself."

"Uh-huh. And I understand. I, uh, I talk to myself, too." She made a gargling noise that might have been a laugh. "You get the best answers that—"

"Do I look like a fool?"

"Ah…"

"Do I look like the type of man who needs to hit a woman over the head with a club, toss her over my shoulder and carry her back to my cave?"

"No. Oh, no. You most certainly—"

"On the other hand, a woman—one who had reason to do so—could probably entice even the most civilized man into such behavior, if she wished."

"Well, I—"

"She could." Matthew's voice was impatient. Why hadn't he seen the truth before? What had happened was Susannah Madison's doing, not his. She'd stop at nothing for the chance to cut him down to size. Or to hang onto her job. One or the other, maybe both. Who knew? Who cared? What mattered was that he'd figured it out, and just in time.

"Thank you for your help, madam," Matthew said. He flashed a glittering smile and stepped into the elevator.

"Uh…didn't you want to get out? I mean, the car came down. Now it's going to go back up…"

"Madam." Matthew drew himself to his full—and imposing—six feet two inches. "I do not need you to tell me that both the car and I are about to make a return trip." He frowned. "I have business—unfinished business—on the fourteenth floor."

"And I have unfinished business in the lobby," the woman said quickly.

"As you wish," Matthew said politely, and pressed the button. The doors slid shut, the car lurched upward, and he folded his arms and contemplated the ceiling.

That Madison woman had made a fool of him not once, but twice.

Well, she wouldn't get away with it.

Never mind giving *CHIC* four weeks. What for? Why should he lose more money? It was revenge, yes, but so what? The magazine was done for. He'd only come here today for the pleasure of firing Susannah Madison in person. And he'd have done what he'd come to do if it hadn't been for that nonsense in the boardroom. Nonsense the Madison broad had engineered.

Matthew's teeth showed in a feral grin.

Had the woman really believed her silly little seduction scene would keep him from delivering the coup de grace? No way. It was the confusion afterward, when her staff had come bursting in, that had left him groping for an explanation.

Well, Madison and company were about to attend another meeting, and he knew exactly what he'd say this time.

"You're fired, every last one of you, and you can thank the charming Miss Madison for what's happened."

Oh, yes.

Matthew tucked his hands into his pockets and began to whistle. The doors opened, and he stepped briskly from the car.

Five minutes later, he stood on the curb.

He was not smiling or whistling. What he was doing was grinding his teeth.

At least, he thought glumly, he'd made a quick exit, substituting the fire stairs for the elevator. He also had his briefcase and the beginning of a nasty headache, one he suspected was going to take four weeks—four very long weeks—to go away.

A taxi pulled to the curb in response to Matthew's raised hand.

"The Manhattan Towers," he said, "on the park."

The cab edged out into traffic. Matthew sat back, folded his arms and continued glowering.

The idea had seemed so simple. Go back, confront everyone at *CHIC*, and make his announcement.

How could he have known that the receptionist would shriek as if he were Tom Cruise and she were a randy teenager? How could he have guessed she'd come running from behind her desk clutching his briefcase in her arms? That she'd babble about how he'd left it behind, how she'd been about to phone his office and find out where to hand deliver it…except she'd been delayed by the celebration?

"Celebration?" he'd said cautiously, at which point her eyes had turned suspiciously bright.

"Oh, Mr. Romano," she'd said in a wobbly voice. "We're all so grateful for this chance!"

Matthew had cleared his throat. "Actually, ah, Miss—"

"I'm Judy," she'd said through a tear-stained smile. "See, we were all sure the new owner—well, we didn't know it was you, but we figured it would be, you know, off with their heads with one big chop without even giving us a chance to prove ourselves."

"To tell you the truth, Judy—"

"I was so worried. About my mother, you know? She's in the hospital, she fell and broke her leg but it's not too bad, really, she could just as easily have broken her hip again."

"Judy," Matthew had said desperately, "if you'd just give me a minute—"

"Eddie, from the mail room? He called his girlfriend. They were supposed to get married this weekend. She's pregnant, which is great, they wanted this baby, but once he figured he might be out of a job… Anyway, he told her the good news. I mean, we know nothing's permanent but now that you've shown this faith in us and in Susannah…"

Matthew shut his eyes as the cab maneuvered through the crowded streets.

Another minute, she'd probably have credited him with finding the cure for the common cold.

He looked out the window, his expression grim. Unfortunately, Judy had misjudged him. He wasn't a miracle worker. He was CEO of a multimillion-dollar corporation. He was a man who made tough decisions. And so he'd done what any prudent man would have done under the circumstances.

He'd taken the briefcase from Judy's hands, thanked her…and gotten out of there as quickly as possible.

What else could he have done?

"What else?" he muttered wearily.

The cabby glanced in the mirror and smiled happily. "Yes," he said.

Matthew sighed. "Yes," he said.

Why not?

The single word seemed to sum it all up.

It didn't sum anything up for Joe Romano.

Matthew's kid brother was not a yes-man. It was why their working relationship succeeded. Joe called it as he saw it.

He'd watched with respect and occasional awe as Matthew swam through shark-filled waters and came out untouched. And when his big brother pulled off an occasionally outrageous, unpredictable, even dangerous stunt, Joe was the first to applaud.

Matt courted danger. It was part of the reason he'd climbed so far so fast.

But what Matt had just told him wasn't outrageous or unpredictable or dangerous. It was crazy. Okay, they hadn't seen each other for a few days. Joe had been in Boston on business. Luck had brought them together in New York for brunch before they both flew home. Surely, a few days wasn't enough time for Matt to have turned into a crazy man.

For that reason—and, Joe had to admit, for curiosity's sake—he wasn't about to let the topic of Matt's morning meeting slide by.

Joe took a sip of his coffee.

"And?" he asked, smiling a little. "You met with Susan Reagan, saw her staffers and…?"

Matthew picked up his fork, scooped up another piece of his portobello mushroom omelet and gave Joe a benign smile.

"And what? That's all there is to it. I gave *CHIC* four weeks to try to get its act together."

"A month? You gave that excuse for a magazine a month?"

Matthew buttered a biscuit. "Whoever recommended this place was right. They do a terrific brunch."

"Glad you think so. Matt, why'd you give *CHIC* a month?" Joe leaned forward. "I'm trying to get a handle on this deal."

So am I, Matthew thought, and forced a smile to his lips.

"Look, four weeks isn't forever. What's the difference if we close *CHIC* down now or later? The operation's still a write-off."

"I know, but you said you were determined to shut them down today. Did you see something that changed your mind? Facts, figures, projections?"

"No."

"No?"

"We could give *CHIC* four years, and it still wouldn't be a moneymaking proposition."

Joe's brows lifted. "Then why did you give them the month?"

Matthew reached for his coffee and took a sip, savoring it with an intensity he usually reserved for a vintage wine.

"Great coffee," he said briskly. "I wonder if they grind their own beans."

"Matt. Talk to me, will you?"

"About what?"

"About why you flew all the way to New York to shut *CHIC* down in person."

Matthew looked at his brother. "You know why."

"Yeah. The memos. The E-mails. The, ah, the Susan Ford take on Matthew Romano."

"Her name is Susannah Madison," Matthew said coldly. "And don't even let me see your lips twitch. Nothing the woman wrote was the least bit amusing."

"Of course not," Joe said quickly. "That's why I don't understand..." He hesitated. "Wait a minute. You did fire her, didn't you?"

A muscle knotted in Matthew's jaw. "No."

"No? As in, no, you didn't?"

"No, as in I had every intention of dumping her. And of shutting the place down, but—"

"But?"

The brothers stared at each other. But what? Matthew thought. What could he say? That a hellcat in a sweatshirt and jeans had painted him into a corner?

"But," he said calmly, looking at his plate, devoting attention to the omelet he didn't have the appetite to eat, "I changed my mind."

"Because?" Joe said helpfully.

Matthew took his time chewing, swallowing and trying to come up with an answer.

"Because it didn't seem fair to pull the rug out from under all *CHIC*'s employees just so I could get even with one person. Look, what's the difference? She'll be out of our hair in four weeks."

Joe shoved aside his eggs Benedict and looked at his brother.

"I suggested something similar to you, remember? Fold the magazine, give the *CHIC* staffers a month's pay plus benefits. And you said the pay and bennies were fine, but you still wanted to hand the Coolidge dame—"

"Madison," Matthew said sharply. "Her name is Madison."

"Clinton, Madison, Teddy Roosevelt, what does it matter? You wanted to sock it to her in person."

Matthew looked around, caught the eye of their waiter and gestured towards his empty coffee cup.

"So how come you didn't?"

Matthew's expression hardened. "Let's get something straight," he said softly. "You're my brother. And my right-hand man. But I run my own show. I don't answer to anybody, not even you. Got that?"

Joe's eyes narrowed. "Yeah," he said. "Yeah, I've got it."

Oh, hell. Matthew reached out his hand as Joe got to his feet.

"Joe—"

"It's okay, I got the message."

"Joe, for God's sake, sit down."

"What for? You made your point."

"Dammit," Matthew said, through his teeth, "will you sit down?"

The brothers glared at each other and then Joe slid into the booth. Matthew leaned over the table, his eyes flat and cold as stone.

"The woman made a fool of me."

Joe's brows lifted. "How?"

"She—she…" Color flooded Matthew's face. He sat back and reached for his coffee. "Never mind how. The point is, she's not going to get away with it."

"No?"

"No. I can promise you that. Miss Susannah Madison most definitely will not pull this off."

"Pull what off?"

"Let's just say she created a situation that kept me from shutting down the magazine."

Joe leaned in. "What'd she do?"

"It doesn't matter. The point is, it won't work. You can bet on it."

"Can you at least tell me what you plan to do?"

Matthew frowned as the waiter served more coffee along with dessert. When he and Joe were alone again, he picked up a fork, poked at his slice of Chocolate Decadence, put down the fork and shoved the plate aside.

"No chocolate cake?" Joe asked, watching the performance with a puzzled expression.

"Nobody eats chocolate cake for breakfast."

"This is brunch, not breakfast. And you do, all the time." Joe grinned. "Remember that screwed-up blood test, the one that almost lost you that football scholarship because you ate Nonna's chocolate cake for breakfast and ended up with a sugar count that sent the doc into a panic?"

"Yeah, well, I'm not hungry."

"I could see that. You left over half your meal."

Matthew's eyes flashed. "I do not need a keeper, Joe."

"My, oh, my, but you are a joy this morning."

The brothers glared at each other, and then Matthew sighed.

"Hell," he muttered. "I'm sorry. I'm just in a lousy mood."

Joe grinned. "Who'd have guessed?"

"Look, I promise you, I'm going to take care of Susannah Madison. I just want to do it in my own time, in my own way. Okay?"

"Sure. You're the boss. And Madison is your problem."

"Exactly."

Joe tucked into his cherry Danish, Matthew into his Chocolate Decadence.

"She put me in a difficult position," he said, after a moment's silence.

"Susannah Madison?"

"Yes."

Joe frowned and looked up. "That must have taken some doing."

Matthew nodded glumly. "Tell me about it," he said bitterly.

"What'd she do?"

It was a good question. When you came right down to it, what *had* she done, except respond to something he'd started? Matthew frowned. No. He hadn't started it. He couldn't have. He'd never in his life come on to a woman in such a frenzy. And, hell, if he ever did, it wouldn't be to a woman like Madison.

"Matt? What'd she do?

"Nothing."

Joe started to reply, thought better of it and waited.

"Nothing I can explain," Matthew said after a minute. "She just... It's complicated."

"So I see. Well, at least tell me what she's like."

"She's..." Matthew poked the tines of his fork into his cake. "She's female."

"Yeah, I figured that out for myself. What's she look like? A dried-up prune? A dog? An old maid on the wrong side of forty?"

Matthew shrugged, gave up pretending he had the appetite for the cake and pushed the plate away.

"She's younger than that."

"Thirty-five?"

"Younger."

"But shriveled?"

Matthew shrugged again. "Not exactly shriveled."

"But not a looker."

"Not exactly a looker, no."

"A woofer?"

"Not exact— Dammit, Joe, what's the difference?"

"Calm down, will you? You can't blame me for being curious."

"Yeah." Matthew sighed. "Sorry. It's just that…"

"You're in a lousy mood. Well, who wouldn't be, after a morning spent in the clutches of a cunning female?"

Matthew's head jerked up. "What's that supposed to mean? A morning spent… Did I say anything about being clutched?"

"Whoa," Joe said, holding up his hands. "I think we've got a communication problem, big brother."

Matthew glared across the table. Joe glared right back, and finally Matthew began to laugh.

"This is ridiculous. You, me, arguing—and over what?"

"Yeah," Joe said quietly. "That's a good question."

"Look, let's get out of here." Matthew twisted in his seat, caught their waiter's eye and signaled for the check. "Phone La Guardia while I take care of this. Make sure the plane's standing by. The sooner we get back to L. A. the better."

"Agreed." Joe took his cell phone from his pocket. "Matt? You're sure you're okay?"

Matthew nodded. "I'm sure. It was—it was an interesting morning. Susannah Madison threw me off base for a couple of minutes, but—"

"Who'd have guessed?" Joe said, in a dry tone that made Matthew grin.

"Look, I'll give you all the details some day. For now, get that worried look off your face. I'll cut the woman down to size, just as soon as—"

The phone rang.

"Mine," Matthew said, and reached into his pocket for his cell phone. "Yes?" He listened intently, his expression darkening. "Dammit, Jane, why did you…" Bloody hell. Susannah Madison had struck again. How could he lay the blame on his secretary? The woman's victims were everywhere. "Sorry, Jane. You did the right thing. No, that's fine. I'll handle it."

Joe watched as Matthew slid the phone into his pocket.

"Problem?" he finally asked, looking at Matthew's stony face.

"That was Jane."

"I heard. What's so important in L.A. that she had to call you here?"

The waiter put down the check. Matthew scrawled his name and waved it away.

"The Madison woman called my office."

"Just now?"

"She said she'd forgotten to give me some important documents. Jane told her where to find me."

"You mean, Madison is sending a messenger here?"

Matthew looked up, his eyes almost black with anger.

"Apparently, she's going to deliver them in person. And believe me, Joe, there aren't any documents, important or otherwise. That woman and I said all we needed to say a couple of hours ago."

"Well, then, what's she want?"

"I don't know."

Joe gave a soft whistle. "I was right. This is definitely one cunning broad."

Matthew got to his feet. "I'm almost tempted to wait just so you can get a look at her." He gave a short, sharp laugh. "You wouldn't believe it unless you saw it."

Joe rose, too. "I knew it," he said, and chuckled. "She's a bow wow after all, right?"

"I cannot tell a lie." Matthew clapped his brother on the back. "Too bad I'm not willing to hang around so you can— Joe? What's the matter?"

"Man, oh, man," Joe said softly. "Don't look now, but there is a definite babe coming up right behind you."

Matthew grinned. "A babe, huh?"

"A ten, if ever I saw one. New York at its best. Gorgeous face. Eyes to drown in. Hair that looks as if some guy just ran his fingers through it. A body that won't quit, and legs that are unbelievable, all packed into a little black suit and a pair of high heels…"

"Mr. Romano?"

Matthew froze. That voice. Those cold, clipped tones. *Please,* he thought, *oh please, don't let it be who I think it is.*

"Mr. Romano," the voice said again.

Matthew's eyes met Joe's. Joe raised a brow.

"It's the babe," Joe mouthed.

Matthew groaned. "No," he said, as he turned, "no, it can't be."

But it was.

The babe—and Joe was right, there was no other word to describe her—the babe was Susannah Madison.

CHAPTER FIVE

MATTHEW took a step back.

This couldn't be Susannah Madison. It couldn't be.

Where had happened to the trick-or-treat hairdo? The grab-bag chic? For that matter, he thought wildly, what had happened to his jaw?

It was touching his shoe tops.

Well, why wouldn't it? The woman standing before him was...

"Gorgeous," Joe said softly.

Yes, she was. From the top of her head to the tips of her toes. Matthew's head spun. She was gorgeous, all right, and everything in between was nothing short of that overworked word, spectacular.

Joe dug an elbow into Matthew's ribs. "Close your mouth," he whispered.

Matthew did.

"And introduce me."

Introduce him? Matthew thought wildly. Smile and say, "Joe, this is Susannah Madison"?

Not in this lifetime. Not unless he was ready to be fitted for one of those jackets with the arms that tied in the back, because how on earth was he going to explain that the woman he'd agreed was a dog, a prune, a woofer, was the same woman who stood before him now?

Only a fairy godmother with one heck of a lot of influence could have waved her wand and accomplished this. Susannah Madison was beautiful. There was no other word to describe her.

Matthew's gaze flew over her again, taking in all the details. A black suit had replaced the Beethoven sweatshirt and the baggy jeans. The suit was demure, even severe, but it couldn't disguise the curves beneath.

Black shoes had replaced the sneakers. Not just any black

shoes. Matthew swallowed hard. The heels were high. Not outrageously high. They were surely some Fifth Avenue shop's idea of dress-for-success shoes to match the dress-for-success suit, but high enough to show off the trimness of Susannah's ankles and the luscious length of her legs. And they were cut low enough in the front so he could see…what did you call those little lines between a woman's toes? Cleavage?

He wanted to laugh—the word, the very concept, seemed so outrageous—but how could he laugh when he was busy concentrating on keeping his jaw from dropping again?

His gaze skittered to her face. She'd done something to it. Not much. Lipstick, maybe. That was all, but the hint of color brought out the sexy tilt of her mouth. Joe had described her hair with dangerous accuracy. It looked as if a man had just run his hands through it. And, dammit, if that man's name was Peter, the SOB was in for a very bad time.

"Ahem," Joe said loudly.

Matthew struggled to gather his scrambled thoughts. Could a touch of lipstick and a change of clothes do all this?

The answer came with heart-stopping swiftness.

Susannah Madison had always looked like this. Always—including that fateful moment when she'd walked into the boardroom. He hadn't forgotten to wear his brain this morning, he'd just been so damned angry he hadn't taken the time to put it into gear. But another part of his anatomy, the one that was located further south, had noticed what she looked like, all right, and had gone into instant overdrive.

Matthew shuddered.

So, there was good news and bad news. At least now he knew he hadn't gone round the bend, hadn't hit on a woman who was, to use Joe's delicate phrase, a woofer. That was the good news. The bad was that he'd been led on by that primal part of himself that was the least dependable decision maker ever invented.

And Madison knew it, knew it so well that she'd come after him again. She was loaded for bear this time. She'd taken the trouble to go home, change into an outfit that had every man within hailing distance salivating…including his pitiful brother.

"Matt," Joe said, "aren't you going to introduce us?"

Matthew ignored him.

"Miss Madison," he said coldly. "How unfortunate to see you again."

Joe twitched. "Madison?" he whispered. "Susannah Madison?"

"The very same," Matthew said, his eyes locked on Susannah's.

Joe cleared his throat. "Well," he said, "well, well, well."

Matthew shot him an angry look. "The plane, remember?"

"Uh-huh." Joe grinned, stepped beside Matthew and put out his hand. "It's a pleasure, Miss Madison. I'm Matt's brother, Joe, and, ah, and he's told me a lot about you."

Susannah, who had been staring at Matthew Romano, switched her gaze to the second man. What, exactly, did *that* mean? What had the detestable Mr. Romano said? If he'd talked about what had happened in the boardroom, she'd have bet anything he hadn't been honest, hadn't told his brother—who looked like a very nice man—that he'd taken advantage of the situation to confuse, intimidate and infuriate her so he could come on to her.

Because that was what he'd done, all right. Taken advantage. Otherwise, he'd never have been gotten away with kissing her. And she'd never have responded. Not that she *had* responded. Why would she? She'd been kissed before, caressed before...

But not driven wild before, she thought, and she felt the color race into her face.

Stop that, she told herself fiercely, and took Joe's outstretched hand.

"I'll make a deal with you, Mr. Romano," she said, with a cool smile. "If you'll remember to discount ninety-nine percent of whatever your brother said, I won't hold it against you that you and he are related."

Joe laughed with delight. Matthew's eyes narrowed to slits.

"Miss Madison. I'm a busy man. In fact, my brother and I were just—"

"Just about to have a second cup of coffee. Won't you join us?"

"Joe," Matthew said tersely, "we have a plane to catch."

"Matt's such a joker." Joe chuckled as he pulled out a chair. "The plane belongs to him. It doesn't leave until he does. Isn't that right, Matt?"

"Oh, yeah," Matthew said through his teeth. "I just love to joke around." Susannah had already seated herself at the table, and Joe was slipping into his seat, too. He bit back the urge to bark at them both. He'd lost control once today, thanks to this woman. It wasn't going to happen a second time, especially with Joe to witness it. "Okay," he snapped, and sat down, arms folded over his chest. "You've got five minutes to explain what you're doing here."

Susannah nodded. Five minutes was four minutes more than she'd let herself hope for. The question was, where to begin? Everybody at *CHIC* was singing Matthew Romano's praises. Only she knew the man was a gold-plated, icy-hearted rat.

And a rat, even in a suit and tie, would always be a rat.

The staff had gone crazy after he'd left.

"Oh, Suze," Claire had squealed, "Suze, you're a miracle worker! What did you do to convince the man to give us a chance?"

That, she was sure, had been her cue to blush and stammer and make up a story that would cover the fact that he expected her to sleep with him if she wanted the magazine to survive. Did Romano really think she was that desperate? Or that naive? She wouldn't have slept with him if giant bugs from Betelgeuse conquered Earth and he and she were humankind's last chance at survival.

Well, maybe she'd do it, then. After all, there'd be a serious reason to make such a sacrifice, to sleep with a man even if she hated his guts.

Even if he was gorgeous. Susannah's heart gave a little kick. Gorgeous was the word.

Studly.

Still, she'd never sleep with him. She didn't do that kind of thing.

And he would never suggest it.

There were laws against sexual harassment. No matter what else he was, the man was a savvy businessman. One whiff of a scandalous lawsuit and Romano Inc. would be up to its knees in nasty publicity.

So he'd tossed out the four-weeks, she's-made-me-very-happy lifeline for only one reason. To torture her. To make her spend every day of those next weeks knowing, *knowing* the chances he'd change his mind about *CHIC* ranged from zero to none. Her people would hope and dream and work their tails off—and it would all be for nothing. She and the heartless Matthew Romano would be the only ones who knew it.

Standing there, facing Claire and the others, Susannah had realized that it didn't have to be that way. Romano *was* a savvy businessman, and if she could find a way to make *CHIC*'s circulation and advertising rates increase, he'd be a fool to shut it down just to get even with her.

If there was a buck to be made, Romano would want to make it.

All she had to do was find the way. And that's when she'd remembered the idea she'd come up with on the way to work. So she'd phoned his secretary, started to race out the door, remembered how she looked and asked herself if the CEO of a multimillion-dollar firm would pay more attention to a proposal made by a woman wearing jeans and a sweatshirt or one made by a woman dressed like an executive.

The answer had been so obvious it hadn't required any effort at all. What *had* required effort was figuring out how to change clothes without heading all the way downtown, then turning around and heading uptown again. Her only hope had been to cross her fingers and tell everybody a white lie. She said she'd just had a call inviting her to lunch with Romano at his hotel.

"Impressive," Claire had breathed.

"I know," Susannah had answered, "but I have to be there in fifteen minutes, and just look at me."

So, here she was, wearing a black wool suit scrounged from a fashion shoot and a pair of shoes donated by Amy, *CHIC*'s very own fashion maven. The jacket was too snug, the skirt too short, the heels too high, but none of that mattered. What mattered was that she'd made it. She was here, seated opposite a glowering man who probably suspected she'd figured out his game and, by God, she was going to make the most of her allotted five minutes if—

"Three minutes left, Miss Madison."

Joe Romano gave an exaggerated sigh.

"Pay no attention, Susannah. You don't mind if I call you that, do you?"

"No. No, I—"

"I don't believe in formality, do I, Matt?" Joe decided to ignore Matthew's warning look. His big brother was rattled. It was a rare, hell, a unique sight, and he wasn't about to let the opportunity to have a little fun at Matt's expense slip by. "My brother, on the other hand, is always formal. And always polite. He's just not himself today. Are you, Matt?"

"I am completely myself," Matthew said coldly. "And the seconds are ticking away."

Susannah slipped her leather bag from her shoulder. "That's okay," she said. Her hands were icy with fear, and she fumbled at the clasp. "I don't need much time to show you this."

She shoved a notepad across the table. Matthew turned it toward him and looked at it, his brows arcing at the nearly indecipherable scrawls.

"Hieroglyphics? Interesting, but, unfortunately, I am not an Egyptologist."

"Those are project notes," Susannah said politely, even though she ached to shove the notepad up that arrogant, masculine nose. "I'm sorry if you can't make them out, but I wrote them in a rush. I'll be happy to read them to you."

"No," Matthew said.

"Yes," Joe said.

Matthew looked at his brother. "Didn't you have an appointment?"

His tone was calm. It had been known to make recalcitrant bankers turn pale. Unfortunately, it didn't even make Joe blink.

"An appointment? No. How could I? We're going back to L.A., remember?" Joe smiled at Susannah. "Notes for a project for *CHIC*? Sounds interesting. I used to manage a magazine myself, once upon a time."

"It was a college yearbook," Matthew said, through his teeth.

Susannah cleared her throat. "I'm sure that must have been interesting," she said carefully.

"Oh, it was." Joe grinned. "Maybe I could help you develop this plan, whatever it is, for your magazine. I've got time on my hands. My brother doesn't always know what to do with my talents."

"I've got some ideas for your talents that might surprise you," Matthew said grimly. "And the lady doesn't have a magazine. I have it, and I'm not interested in doing anything but putting it out of its misery."

"That's what my notes are all about, Mr. Romano." Susannah took a deep breath. "I've come up with an idea that will turn CHIC around."

Matthew laughed. "Only Houdini could turn CHIC around, Miss Madison. Or are you telling me those are notes you took at a séance?"

"CHIC used to be the top-selling magazine for women between the ages of eighteen and thirty-five," Susannah said, refusing to rise to the bait. She picked up the notepad, flipped a page and tapped her fingers against it. "Just look at these circulation figures. There's not a publication in the country that wouldn't kill for numbers like those."

Matthew dismissed the page with a glance. "Those numbers are five years old," he said. "They have no relevance."

"But they do! We lost those readers because we went in the wrong direction. American women in the target age group lead busy lives, Mr. Romano. They have jobs, husbands, children. They don't want recipes that take two hours to prepare and they don't need hints on how to vacuum their way to happiness."

"Do you really think this is news, Miss Madison?"

"They want features that make them forget their troubles, if only for a while. Fantasy, Mr. Romano. Fantasy, that's what they want. They want to read about—about Venice by moonlight. They want recipes for candlelit suppers even if the reality is that they're going to end up ordering in pizza."

"Fascinating," Matthew said, in a way that sent Susannah's blood pressure skyrocketing. "There is a diversity of readers—and, I'm certain, a diversity of magazines on the market. If you're going to suggest CHIC join their ranks—"

"The diversity is the problem, Mr. Romano."

Matthew shot his cuff and looked pointedly at his watch.

"As I said, this is fascinating, but I have a dinner appointment on the coast, and—"

"I believe I can double our readership and our advertising revenue by focusing on the one common interest they all share."

"Your time is up, Miss Madison." Matthew pushed back his chair and rose. "Joe?"

Joe sighed and looked at Susannah. "Sorry," he said, "but when Matt's right—"

"Sex," she blurted.

There was a sudden silence in their vicinity. Matthew glared around him, glared at Susannah and sat down again.

"I should have expected this," he growled. "Listen, lady, whatever happened in that boardroom—"

"Wow," Joe said, and grinned. "In the boardroom?"

Matthew shot him a withering glance. "One more word, you can walk back to L.A."

"Sex sells," Susannah said, hurrying the words, wondering if she'd manage to get through this before the Romano brothers went for each other's throats. "It sells cars and toothpaste and beer. It sells everything."

The men looked from each other to her. "So?" Matthew said.

"So," Susannah said, folding her hands in her lap to keep them from shaking, "so, it can sell *CHIC*."

"How?" Matthew offered a pitying smile. "All the women's magazines are pushing sex. There's nothing new about that."

A smile curved across her mouth, one so smug it made him want to haul her to her feet and—

"You're getting ahead of me," she said. "What do you know about magazine publishing, Mr. Romano?"

"Not much. But I know enough about balance sheets to tell you that you're wasting my time."

"Do you read any? Magazines, I mean."

Matthew's eyes narrowed. Susannah had to concentrate on not leaping to her feet and racing for the door.

"I know this will astound you," he said gently, "but I can, with some effort, manage to recite the alphabet all the way from A to Z."

Bastard! Did he think this was amusing? Susannah took a breath.

"Then I'll rephrase my question, since I doubt you expend all the energy it must take to decode periodicals that would be of interest to our target reader."

Joe laughed. Matthew looked at him.

"Joe?" The single word seemed to float above the table, shimmering with meaning.

"Yes?"

"I'll meet you at La Guardia."

Joe shrugged, smiled lazily and got to his feet. "Good idea. Actually, bro, I think you need to handle this, ah, this situation on your own." He smiled, reached for Susannah's hand and, when she gave it to him, brought it to his lips. "It's been a pleasure, Susannah. And an education. I certainly hope we'll see each other again."

"Not in this lifetime," Matthew muttered as his brother strolled away. He caught the eye of the worried-looking waiter and signaled for coffee. After it had been poured, he moved his chair closer to the table. "All right, Miss Madison." His tone and his expression were grim. "You seem determined to have some sort of showdown, so let's get to it."

"No showdown," Susannah said quickly. She leaned forward, her eyes on his. "Picture this. A woman—let's call her Mary Anne—works hard all day, comes home at night to an empty apartment, pulls a TV dinner from the freezer, curls up on the sofa, watches TV..."

"I fail to see what this hypothetical Mary Lou has to do with—"

"Mary Anne. Mary Lou's her sister. Mary Lou spends the day doing laundry and running after the kids. At night, she stirs up some leftovers for dinner, cleans up the kitchen, then joins her husband in front of the television set. It's Monday night. He's watching football. She watches for a little while and then she yawns and goes to—"

"Bed," Matthew said impatiently. "So?"

"What's the common factor missing from both their lives, Mr. Romano?"

"How in hell should I know?" Matthew asked irritably. Was that what Susannah Madison did with her nights? Go home, eat a frozen dinner, curl up on the sofa and watch TV? No. He'd left something out of the equation. Susannah ate her dinner with a man named Peter. She curled up on the sofa with him, watched TV with him, went to bed with him...

"Romance," Susannah said, and gave him that same smug smile again.

Matthew blinked away the red haze that had formed in front of his eyes. "I beg your pardon?"

"Don't you see?" Her voice rose with excitement. "Both those women—those potential readers—are desperate for some romance in their lives. Fantasy, remember? *CHIC* can give it to them and, once it does, the advertisers of everything from soap to soup will be clamoring for space in the magazine."

"Is this a new takeoff on those perfume-strip inserts they put into magazines nowadays, Miss Madison? You know— open *CHIC*, turn to page thirty-seven and there's a strip labeled Moonlight and Flowers?"

"Turn to page thirty-seven," Susannah said eagerly, "and there's a recipe for Lobster bisque a deux."

"Lobster bisque for—"

"For two."

"I know what the phrase means, dammit! I just don't see—"

"And two pages later, there's a feature article on the language of perfume."

Lobster? The language of perfume? And what had she meant about him being ahead of her when he'd made that crack about sexy magazines? If she had a plan, he couldn't see it. Not that it mattered. Nothing she could say would change his mind about the folly of throwing good money after bad.

But, dammit, she was even more lovely to look at now, with her cheeks pink and rosy and her eyes glittering with excitement.

Matthew frowned and cleared his throat. "I'm, ah, I'm afraid I've never heard of the language of—"

"Perfume. What scents are sexier to a man? Florals? Greens? Orientals?"

He blinked. "Well, I—I—" *Whatever it is you're wearing,* he thought, and he knew suddenly that it was time to put this conversation to rest. "Miss Madison." He spoke gently. He could see, after all, that she'd put some effort into this. It wasn't her fault her plan wasn't any good. "Susannah," he said, in an even more kindly fashion, "I'm sure you've put a lot of thought into these suggestions, but—"

"There'll be a contest each month, and wonderful prizes."

"Contest?" Matthew frowned. "What kind of contest? I've seen the contests women's' magazines run. Best dessert recipe. Best main course. I thought you said—"

"And I thought you said you didn't read women's magazines."

"I don't. Read women's magazines, I mean. But I'm not dead. I see the covers on the stands."

"Then you know that there are enough contests like that to last a lifetime." Susannah lifted her chin. "Our contests will ooze romance. Well, we won't say 'romance,' we'll say 'sexiest.' Because sex—"

"Sells. So you've already pointed out. Sexiest what, then? Meat loaf?"

Damn the man! Was he being deliberately dense? His smile was so condescending it made her want to slug him. Instead, she gave a trilling laugh, as if to show him she knew he was joking.

"Sexiest movie, Mr. Romano. Or—or sexiest way to spend an afternoon." She saw the first faint glimmer of interest in his blue eyes. Her heart lifted because she'd caught his attention—and her palms grew damp because the worst was yet to come. "The possibilities are endless," she said. "Sexiest city in America, sexiest restaurant in New York…"

"Why limit it? Take a global approach, appeal to a wide cross-section of women. Sexiest city in the world. Sexiest restaurant in the world. Don't you agree that would be better?"

"Yes," she said, trying not to bounce up and down in her seat because now she had him.

"No."

Susannah jerked back in shock. "No?"

"That's what I said. No."

"But you said…you just said…"

"It's an idea. An interesting idea, but a monthly feature like the one you're describing wouldn't have sustained appeal. It has no real focus. One month, two, three, and readers would start to drift.''

He was right, of course, and she *did* have a focus. She was about to lay it out for him—which was definitely a poor choice of words, all things considered. All she had to do was make him see the logic to her plan. Perhaps he would. Perhaps she hadn't given him enough credit for creative thinking. Actually—actually, the way he was looking at her, with all his attention focused on her and his blue eyes narrowed and thoughtful, she could see that some people might get the idea Matthew Romano was an intelligent, capable man. An intelligent, capable man who was rising to his feet and smiling in polite dismissal.

''I'll still give you four weeks, Miss Madison, but—''

''*CHIC* will run a monthly feature.'' She scrambled from her chair and hurried after him to the door. ''Readers will send in their favorite choices for the sexiest whatever of the month. Wine, city, restaurant…and whoever wins will get the particular thing they voted for. A case of vintage wine. A late supper for two. A weekend in Paris.''

''Nice,'' Matthew said, trying to concentrate on what she was saying and not on the feel of her hand or the smell of her hair. ''But—''

''But where does it lead? What's its focus?'' Susannah swallowed dryly. ''To—to February. The Valentine's Day issue, when we name the Sexiest Man Alive and feature him as our centerfold.''

Oh, damn! There it was, out in the open. And there *he* was, turning to stone right before her eyes, stepping back on the sidewalk and giving her a look so icy she felt the chill of it in her bones.

''And so we come full circle, Miss Madison,'' he said coldly. ''Tell me, did you work all this out just so you could remind me of how your name first came to my attention, or did you think that some miraculous whim of fate would have erased it from my memory?''

''Mr. Romano—''

''Goodbye, Miss Madison,'' Matthew said, and marched to the curb. Where was a taxi when you needed one?

''Mr. Romano, wait a minute!''

He swung around, eyes glittering. "You believe in living dangerously," he said softly.

"I believe in honesty. And that's why I'm telling you this would work."

Matthew turned away from her. "Taxi?" He stepped off the curb as a yellow cab swerved toward the sidewalk. "La Guardia Airport," he said, as he climbed in.

Susannah climbed in after him.

"This conversation is finished, Miss Madison."

"Mr. Romano, please…"

"Go ahead, driver." Matthew sat back, arms folded, eyes fixed straight ahead as the cab pulled into the road.

"Mr. Romano." Susannah licked her lips. "Why did you notice that—that item in my note to Claire?"

Matthew didn't so much as blink.

"I'll tell you why," she said quickly. "Because it was about sex. That's why. And because it was just the opposite of what we're accustomed to. You know, a woman considering a man as—as…"

"Oh, don't lose courage now, Miss Madison." Matthew looked at Susannah. A hard, dangerous smile edged across his mouth. "Man as what?"

"As—as a desirable sexual object."

"Do you really think a man—any man—would wish to have himself described that way? Featured in a magazine, yet?" He leaned closer, and she shrank back in the seat. "No, a man would not. He'd be offended. Our readers would be offended."

"Burt Reynolds."

"I beg your pardon?"

"Burt Reynolds. The movie star. He was a centerfold, years and years ago. It did wonders for his career and for the magazine that featured him as their centerfold."

"I doubt," Matthew said frigidly, "if Burt Reynolds is interested in posing for *CHIC*."

"No. Of course not. But that's just my point. We'd search for an actor. A model. Men who're accustomed to being in front of the public. And we'll check with each one of them before we offer them to our readers as choices."

"Choices," Matthew grumbled. "Sounds like you're talking about a menu. One from this column, one from that..."

It also sounded wacky. Wacky enough, perhaps, to work.

Susannah touched his arm. "I can make it work. I know I can."

Her hand lay lightly on his arm, yet he could feel the heat of her fingertips burning into his flesh. Ridiculous, he told himself. But his body was already hardening, as if the feel of her, hot and silken in his arms, was embedded in his memory.

"It's out of the question," he said brusquely. "Even if there were a chance in a million your plan would work, I'd have to pour money into a dying magazine. There's no logic in that."

"Not so much money," Susannah said quickly. "We already have the staff."

"Do you have the budget for sending your contest winners to Paris, Miss Madison?"

"I can squeeze the money out of something else."

"Ha."

"I can! I wouldn't do a thing without your approval. I'd fax you every day."

"There's a three-hour time difference between L.A. and New York. By the time you faxed me something, you'd already have done it."

"Put someone in charge, then. A publisher. You already have one, don't you? I mean, Update *is* yours, isn't it?"

"Update publishes pharmaceutical journals. The gentleman in charge is pushing eighty."

Her face fell. "Oh."

"Oh, indeed." *Why did she have to look at him as if he were the only man who could save the world from imminent disaster?*

"Your brother," Susannah said.

"Joe?" Matthew's brows knotted. "What about him?"

"He said he's underutilized. Couldn't you put him in charge?"

"No."

"Six months. Just give us six months!"

"Forget it. It's a crazy idea."

"Three months, then. Well, three issues. December, January, February."

"Are you deaf, Miss Madison? I said—"

"I read an article about you in *Business Daily* while I was on my way to your hotel." Susannah sat on the edge of her seat and turned toward him. "It said you were a man who took risks, that you could see opportunity where others didn't."

"Revising your opinion of me?" he asked coolly. "Too bad you didn't read that article before you took to passing notes like some junior high school kid."

"Too bad you let personal grudges come between you and a good business decision."

"I never make anything but rational business decisions."

"Make this one, then," Susannah said, her face flushed with determination.

Suddenly, there was a screech of brakes. The cab swerved and jolted to a halt. Susannah slid into Matthew's arms.

"All right," he said.

Susannah blinked. "All right? You mean—"

"I'll give you your three issues, but if *CHIC*'s not in the black by February, I'll pull the plug the day after the Valentine's issue hits the stands."

A smile spread over her mouth. It was, he thought, a lovely mouth.

"Oh, that's wonderful. Thank you, Mr. Romano."

"Matthew. All things considered, we might as well be on a first-name basis, don't you think?"

Susannah laughed. "Yes. Fine. Thank you, Matthew. Thank your brother for me, too." She laughed again, and Matthew couldn't help smiling. "Not that he knows he's been drafted. Not that we can be sure he'll be happy about his new assignment. Not that—"

"It isn't his new assignment."

The smile faded from her face. "But—but you just said..."

"It's simpler if I take the helm."

He hadn't intended to say those words, but now that he had, the idea made sense. He had business in New York that would keep him flying back and forth over the next couple of months, anyway.

All in all it was an excellent idea—and it had nothing, absolutely nothing, to do with Susannah, or with the way Joe had looked at her, or with somebody named Sam, or with Peter, whoever in hell he was.

"Do you have a problem with that?" he asked, very calmly.

Susannah looked at him. Her heart gave a fluttery kick. Matthew Romano, underfoot until February? Matthew Romano, taking up residence in her life?

"No," she said, "No, not at all."

He nodded. "In that case, there's just one last thing..."

And, because it would have been easier for the taxi to have sprouted wings than to have prevented what happened next, Matthew pulled Susannah into his arms and crushed her mouth beneath his.

CHAPTER SIX

WHAT kind of a man kissed a woman he didn't like with such passion?

A better question was, what kind of woman kissed him back? And she was kissing him. There was no point in pretending otherwise.

Matthew was feasting on her mouth, and she was on fire for him, for his kisses and his touch.

Some still logical part of her fought for sanity.

"No," she said, against his mouth, "Matthew, we can't..."

He tunneled his fingers into her hair, tilted her face to his.

"Just kiss me," he said thickly, "kiss me and stop thinking."

She did.

He felt her surrender in the sudden thrust of her body against his, in the erotic little sigh that feathered from her lips. He shifted her in his arms, drew her across his lap. He was hungry, starving for her. She was trembling with need. Her arousal had heated her skin, had made her flesh smell of flowers and springtime. And he—he was as close as he'd ever been to losing everything he was in a woman's arms.

The realization might have stopped him, but then Susannah moved, lifted herself to him, framed his face between her hands, and it was too late.

It was his undoing.

Matthew groaned, parted her lips with his, tilted her head and angled his mouth over hers, deepening the kiss. He caught her bottom lip between his teeth, sucked on the soft flesh, bit lightly and then soothed the wound with the tip of his tongue.

"Susannah," he breathed, "Susannah." It was all he was capable of saying, of thinking, of feeling.

God, he was on fire!

And so was she.

He slid his tongue into her mouth. She moaned softly and

wound her arms around his neck. His body was rock-hard beneath her. The feel of all that tightly leashed power, the realization that she had done this to him, made the kiss even more exciting.

"Yes?"

Susannah froze. "Matthew?"

"I know, sweetheart." Her yes had been soft. Husky. A little deeper than he'd have expected, but who was he to concern himself with Susannah's tone of voice? "I know. You said, yes. And it's the same for—"

"I didn't say anything," she said, scrambling from his lap. "It was the driver."

The driver.

The driver? Matthew met the cabby's eyes in the mirror and breathed a sigh of relief. This was New York, meaning the guy had barely noticed the gymnastics.

"Yes, please, we are here?"

"We are here, yes," Matthew said, looking out the window at La Guardia Airport. "We certainly are."

"Please? Give airline name?"

Matthew cleared his throat. "Ah..."

Ah? What kind of response was that to a simple question? His brain, on holiday early this morning, now seemed to have packed up and left home for good. How else to explain his actions? His loss of control? Susannah looked as baffled as he felt. She was smoothing her jacket, her hair, her skirt, every now and then shooting him quick glances from under her lashes.

Matthew's mouth thinned.

Anybody who didn't know better would have thought games like this were new for her. But he wasn't anybody. He was the man who'd been the butt of her jokes. Even if he hadn't, just one look at her in that sexy suit, one moment spent with her going wild in his arms would have made it clear Susannah Madison was, to use Joe's favorite description, one hot babe.

Matthew straightened his collar, fixed his tie and ran his hands through his hair.

"Sorry," he said briskly.

Susannah jerked her head toward him. Sorry? The man

sounded as if he were apologizing for—for jostling her elbow instead of for...

Oh, lord.

Maybe she'd lost her mind. It was as good an explanation as any. Why else would she have been crawling all over Matthew Romano in the back seat of a taxi? Matthew Romano, a man she didn't like, a man she'd only met, what, four hours ago?

It was all his fault. She smoothed her skirt again, tried uselessly to drag it over her knees. She was embarrassed, and he was sitting there, the epitome of cool.

How she longed to pop him one right in his square jaw. If he hadn't stormed into her life this morning, turned her existence upside down, if he hadn't hauled her into his arms and kissed her as if the clock had spun backward and he were some tenth-century lord of the manor...

She swung toward him. He swung toward her. They stared at each other. Susannah could feel the angry, indignant words building inside her, but How dare you? wasn't really appropriate to the occasion, considering—*Be honest, Susannah*—considering that she'd just been sucking on his tongue.

Color flooded her face.

"Susannah," he said, "that was—it was inappropriate behavior."

She nodded. "It certainly was."

"But it's probably just as well we got it out of the way."

Her eyes widened. "I beg your pardon?"

"I'm sure neither of us wants to muddy the waters with, ah, with a personal involvement."

Bloody hell! What was wrong with him? He sounded like a pimply-faced kid trying to convince his girlfriend that he'd still respect her despite what had happened in the back seat of his Chevy.

"Look," he said, waving his hand, "why don't we forget that, ah, that anything—that we ever..."

"It was a mistake," Susannah said.

"Yes."

"Yes?"

Matthew looked up. The driver was smiling helpfully into the mirror.

"No. I mean, not you, driver. I mean... It was a mistake, yes," he said, turning back to Susannah. "A huge one. And I apologize for my part in it."

Susannah stared at him. It wasn't much of an apology. In fact, it was pretty insulting. It suggested that she'd been as responsible for that kiss as he was. Well, he was right. She was equally responsible, heaven only knew why, but if he was willing to put the kiss behind them, so was she. She took a breath, puffed it out and nodded.

"I agree."

"Good." Matthew smiled politely, thought of shaking Susannah's hand, thought of what might happen if he touched her and frowned. "Good," he said again, and then he leaned forward. "Driver? We've had a change of plans. Take us back into the city, please, to the Manhattan Towers Hote—''

"Absolutely not!"

Susannah was looking at him as if he'd turned into something loathsome right before her eyes.

"You are really something!"

Matthew sighed. He had the feeling she hadn't meant that as a compliment.

"Is there a problem, Miss Madison?"

"Is there a—" Susannah laughed. "Goodbye, Mr. Romano. I'd sooner sell sweaters in Macy's than go back to your hotel with you."

"Macy's? Yes?"

It was the driver again. Matthew shot him a fierce look.

"Macy's, no," he snapped, his voice growing testy.

"Macy's, Lord and Taylor's, the moon," Susannah said, reaching past him to the door.

Matthew clamped his hand on hers. "What the devil are you talking about?"

"I'm talking about the perks of the job. You never mentioned that along with health insurance and a pension plan, I could also count on being tucked into your bed!"

"Are you nuts?"

"Let go of me, Romano."

"Susannah—"

"Don't you 'Susannah' me!"

"Sorry," he said, and tried not to laugh at her tone of righteous indignation. "I figure, once a woman's crawled all over a man, he can assume they're on a first-name basis."

"I'm sure this is very amusing to you, but I find nothing laughable in this situation."

"You will when you calm down enough to listen."

"Let go of my hand, please. I'll take the subway to the office."

"You do that. Just be sure and let me know which runway the train stops at."

"Go ahead, laugh. See if I care."

"It's a long walk back to Manhattan."

"I'll take a taxi," she said, with dignity.

"Dammit, woman, you're in a taxi. Stop being an idiot."

"You stop hanging on to my wrist, or you'll be reading your dentist's estimate for a new set of teeth!"

Matthew laughed. "I'm shaking in my shoes. Now, sit back and take it easy."

"After you just—after what you just—"

"You've got your pronouns wrong, haven't you? I didn't just. We just. Remember the old saying, Susie? It takes two."

Susannah jerked her hand free. "A gentleman would not even suggest such a thing."

"I never said I was a gentleman."

"And a good thing. Otherwise, I'd have to call you a liar as well as a—a cad."

He knew it wasn't fair, teasing her like this. It was just that watching her react—the color that shot into her cheeks, the angry tilt of her head—made it difficult to resist.

But resist he would. He'd resist kissing her again, too, though he had to admit it was going to be tough. Who'd have dreamed Susannah Madison would be so complex? She'd gone from hoyden to businesswoman to sexy siren in less time than it took some women to dress for dinner. And right now, she was doing a credible job of playing the wronged innocent.

Matthew's body tightened.

No question, it would be fun to explore all those layers. But he wasn't interested. This was business, and he never mixed business with pleasure. Besides, he didn't like the woman. And if there was one thing he never did, it was sleep with a woman he didn't like.

Not that she'd ever believe such a thing.

Matthew's brows knotted. Who cared if she did or didn't? The only thing she had to believe was that what had just happened would never happen again.

"You've made a mistake," he said.

Susannah rolled her eyes. "Tell me something I don't know."

"I wasn't asking you back to my hotel," he said briskly.

"No?"

"No. I was simply telling the driver to take us back into Manhattan, now that our plans have changed."

"Ah," the driver said. "Yes, Manhattan?"

Matthew looked into the mirror. "Manhattan, no," he said, as calmly as he could. "When we decide where we want to go, we'll tell you. Okay?"

"Yes. Okay."

Susannah's mouth thinned. The driver sounded about as convinced as she felt. "I'll just bet your plans have changed, Mr. Romano."

"Dammit," Matthew said, "it was just a kiss, that's all. No big deal." She didn't answer, didn't look at him...didn't protest his description. For some reason he couldn't understand, that annoyed the hell out of him.

"You're right," she said, after a minute, "it was no big deal at all."

That annoyed him even more.

"Really," he said.

Susannah looked at him and hoped he couldn't read the truth in her eyes, that nothing she'd ever experienced had been remotely like that kiss.

"Really," she said, with a bored little smile.

Matthew nodded. "So," he said, very calmly, "the guy who plays cards with your mother kisses you like that?"

Color flamed in her cheeks. "I beg your pardon?"

"I'm talking about Sam. The guy who plays cards with your mother instead of making love to you."

"You have absolutely no right to ask me such a—"

"What about Peter? The one you sent kisses to when you were away."

"Peter?" she said, her voice rising. "*Peter?* What do you know about—"

"Answer the question, Madison. Do you kiss him the way you just kissed me?"

Susannah made a strangled sound. *Peter's a cat, Mr. Romano,* she wanted to say, just to see him turn purple. But instinct told her to keep that bit of information to herself.

"How I kiss Sam, or—or Peter, or anybody else, is none of your business."

He nodded. She was right. He knew that. She could kiss a hundred guys from here to the coast. She could make those same little sounds she'd made with him, part her mouth for a hundred other men the same as she'd done for him, get hot in a hundred other pairs of arms. It didn't matter.

"You're right."

"You're damn right, I'm right," she said huffily.

There was a beat of silence, and then Matthew cleared his throat.

"Here's the deal," he said brusquely. "Your plan has merit, and it'll probably do better if you're in charge."

"What do you mean, *if?* It's my plan. Who else could see it through?"

"Someone I'd hire. Don't look so shocked, Madison. It's your plan, but it's my magazine. On that basis, assuming you can file what just happened under F for Forgotten, we go ahead with it."

Susannah linked her hands together in her lap. "I think I should tell you that I really dislike you, Mr. Romano."

"You're breaking my heart."

"You're an arrogant and heartless man."

Matthew sighed, crossed his legs and swung one foot back and forth. "Yes or no, please. Do you want the job? We don't have all day."

"Of course I want it," she snapped. "But I wish I'd never set eyes on you."

"You mean, you wish you'd never kissed me."

Her eyes met his in cold defiance. "Kiss?" she said. "What kiss? It never happened, remember?"

"Exactly." Matthew leaned forward and tapped the partition between the cabby and his passengers. "Driver? Take us into Manhattan, please."

The driver sat up straight. "Yes?" he said happily.

"Yes. Drop the lady off first, at Fortieth and Third, and then take me to the Manhattan Towers Hotel." Matthew sat back, sighed and shook his head. "All this fuss for a kiss."

"We just agreed that there was no kiss."

"Right. Right. There was no kiss."

"Exactly."

Susannah folded her arms. Matthew folded his.

"I don't get involved with women I do business with," he said, as the taxi headed for the tunnel linking Manhattan to Queens.

"Good," Susannah said, staring straight ahead. "That way, you wouldn't have to be disappointed when I turned you down."

"I just think we should be honest, that's all. Admit the attraction. You want to sleep with me, I want to sleep with you, but sex is sex and business is business, and the two don't mix so we're not going to do anything about it. End of story."

Susannah shot him an ugly look. "You cannot imagine how much I loathe you!"

"Great word, loathe. It has so much passion to it." Matthew's smile was as smug as his voice. "Loathe me all you like. That doesn't mean you don't want me."

"Want you? I'd sooner want a snake."

"Yeah?"

"Yeah."

"Well, considering what was going on here a little while ago, you're going to make some snake a very happy reptile."

Susannah swung toward him, her hands knotted into fists. Any second now, she was going to lose her chance at *CHIC*, probably her chance at anything, because once she slugged the horrible Matthew Romano, what would be her chance of getting another job in publishing?

"You really do think you're the sexiest man alive, don't you? Well, let me tell you something, Romano. Just because I was stupid enough to let you kiss me—"

"She let me kiss her," Matthew said, shaking his head.

"It was just…a physical thing. And I don't believe in physical things." Matthew snorted, and she flashed him an enraged look. "I don't sleep around."

His smile turned cool. "I'm sure Peter and Sam would be delighted to hear it."

"I told you," Susannah said, choking back a gust of crazed laughter, "Peter and Sam are none of your business."

"Your personal life is very much my business, Madison." His tone was crisply professional. "I'm sure there's a morals clause in your contract."

"A what?"

"I'll have my attorneys review it."

"What do you mean, a morals clause?"

What *did* he mean? It was one hell of a fine question.

"You represent *CHIC*," he said, wondering if he sounded as stupid to her as he did to himself. "That means you're expected to maintain a certain degree of morality."

"I'm glad to hear one it's expected of one of us."

"I won't ask you to curtail your current relationships with your—your gentlemen friends, but I will ask you to exercise discretion."

"Discretion," Susannah said, and resumed weighing the value of trading her career for one good sock to that handsome jaw.

"Yes. And while we're on the subject, I think you should know that I'm usually more sophisticated in my attempts to separate a beautiful woman from her clothes."

"Am I supposed to be flattered?"

"I don't know what you're supposed to be." That was certainly the truth. Why was he telling her this? There was no reason he could think of. "I, ah, I just thought you were entitled to know that."

"Thank you." Susannah spoke politely, wondering, with a touch of heat, exactly how he usually did get his women out of their clothes. "So long as we're getting everything out in the open..."

"Yes?"

"I think your presence in the office would undermine my authority."

"You have nothing to worry about. I won't be there. I have

some loose ends to tie up in the northeast over the next week or two.''

"When it comes to making decisions, I'll need free rein."

"Of course. Free rein—within limits."

"That's not free rein," she said, eyes flashing.

"That's how I work, Madison. I consult with my people, I listen, I'll change my mind if they convince me I'm wrong—but I'm the guy in charge. Take it or leave it."

His words were cold, but that was fine with her. So long as they both remembered this was a business arrangement...so long as *he* remembered, she thought, frowning. She certainly would. What had happened between them, that kiss, that trip into the hot, dark wildness of her libido, hadn't meant a thing.

"Madison?"

Susannah blinked. "Yes?"

"Can you accept those terms?"

She nodded. "I can accept them—but I'll need an increased budget for advertising to launch the new campaign."

"Send me a breakdown showing what you need and why, and you'll have it."

"And more staff."

"You drive a hard bargain."

He was laughing at her, and she knew it, but she refused to give him the satisfaction of reacting.

"I mean to," she said coolly.

"Anything else?"

"No."

He nodded. "In that case..."

Her heart stopped. Was he going to try to kiss her even after what he'd said? Try, because she wouldn't let him. Absolutely not. She'd never let—

Matthew reached into his pocket, took out his cell phone and hit a button.

He heard Susannah sigh, and he looked at her while the phone dialed automatically. Amazing. She looked as if she were bored.

Bored? he thought, his eyes narrowing.

And then Joe said hello, and Matthew began talking, explaining in crisp terms that he'd decided to stay on in New York for a while.

And what a job that was, considering that Joe never stopped laughing.

It was amazing what a little infusion of money could do.

Well, no. Susannah finished her chicken salad on rye, extra pickle hold the mayo, lifted her coffee cup to her lips and drank the last mouthful.

Not a little infusion. A big one. Matthew had taken over the role of publisher and he'd delivered on all his promises. He'd put money at *CHIC*'s disposal, added another full-time staffer, arranged for a PR company to promote the magazine's name wherever it might prove useful.

And he'd done all that while keeping to his word.

She hadn't so much as laid eyes on him since that afternoon in the taxi, when he'd dropped her at the *CHIC* offices.

Oh, he kept in touch. By telephone. By fax. By E-mail. But two whole weeks had gone by and he hadn't shown his face, which meant he was serious about business being business.

Which was the way she wanted it.

Of course, it was.

The waitress slid Susannah's check in front of her. She tucked a dollar bill under the edge of her plate, picked up the check and made her way through Ellie's Deli to the cash register.

The cashier gave her a friendly smile. "Haven't seen much of you lately," she said.

Susannah smiled and scooped up her change. "I've been busy."

Busy, indeed.

The sidewalk outside Ellie's was crowded, as always, even though the lunchtime exodus from the surrounding office buildings was pretty much finished.

Susannah glanced up and down the street, then stepped off the curb and hurried across.

She missed having lunch with Claire, but it hadn't been possible lately. Everybody at *CHIC* was busy as a colony of bees, eager to get the Sexiest Restaurant issue on the street. The only reason Susannah had even managed time for lunch away from her desk today was that she'd wanted to check out one of the finalists.

"You're supposed to go to these places in the evenings, Suze," Claire had said. "That's when a restaurant is sexy."

She sighed as she stepped inside the lobby and rang for the elevator.

Claire was right, but Susannah's evenings were spent at the office playing catch-up with all the work she hadn't managed to finish during the day. Anyway, it hadn't worked out. The little restaurant was closed. Open For Dinner, the sign in the window had said.

At the rate she was going, she'd never come up with a winner. And that would be disastrous, since they'd already publicized the feature in last month's *CHIC*.

Claire had suggested that a column by the editor-in-chief would give readers a personalized link to the magazine. Susannah had agreed it was a great idea. She'd talk to readers, share the feelings of one eighteen-to-thirty-five-year-old woman with all the other eighteen-to-thirty-five-year-old women out there. And, in her debut column, she'd announced that *CHIC* was searching for the sexiest restaurant and that she'd personally name and describe it in the very next issue. In the meanwhile, readers could send in postcards, there'd be a draw, and one lucky person would get dinner for two at the winning place.

Susannah stepped into the elevator, pressed the button for fourteen. The car began its slow, creaky ascent.

She knew she was almost in over her head. Three special issues of *CHIC* in three months. It was a lot to pull off, maybe too much, and she hadn't even figured out what the third special issue would be about. Not that it mattered. She wasn't going to get through the first issue. If she lived to be a thousand, she'd never have time to check all six finalists, much less declare one a winner, not unless she figured out how to stretch each day to thirty-six hours instead of a measly twenty-four.

The elevator jerked to a stop on the fourteenth floor. She stepped out. Maybe she ought to phone Matthew. The last time they'd talked, he'd asked her how things were going, and she'd said things were just fine, thank you very much....

Judy wasn't at the reception desk. That wasn't so odd, all by itself, but an unnatural quiet hung in the air. Susannah shrugged off her jacket as she made her way down the hall. Where was everybody? Office after office stood empty.

This was eerie. It had only happened once before, the day Matthew had come barging in.

Laughter rang out from the boardroom. She turned, looked down the hall. The boardroom door stood open. She could see people crowded inside.

"Oh, stop it," she muttered, and marched briskly down the corridor.

Claire spotted her first. "Hi, Suze," she called.

It was the same as last time. The entire staff was there, crowded around the conference table. No. It wasn't the same, not at all, because this time, everybody was smiling.

And, this time, when she looked at the man standing at the head of the table, her heart turned over.

"Hi," Matthew said, as he rose to his feet.

"Hi," Susannah said, because it was logical and polite, and because it was safer to be logical and polite than to think about how wonderful it was to see him again, or how it made her feel when his eyes swept over her and his smile warmed.

She extended her hand, and he took it. His grip was firm, his fingers hard and strong, and she wondered how it was that she'd never thought of a handshake as a sensual experience until now. *Say something,* she told herself frantically, but what was there to say except what she could never afford to say, that she knew now that she'd missed him these past weeks?

"Suze," her secretary said, "I hope you don't mind, but when Mr. Romano—"

"Matt," he said.

"Sorry." Pam smiled happily. "When Matt stopped by and I told him you weren't in, and he said, well, he'd just say hello to everybody anyway, well, I just figured the easiest way was to call everybody to the conference room and—"

Pam? Matthew thought. Yeah, that was the name of Susannah's secretary. Pam was going on and on, explaining how this impromptu meeting had come to take place. She was starting to stammer, and he knew it was because neither he nor Susannah were saying anything, knew, too, that he ought to come to the woman's rescue. The *CHIC* staff was gathered here instead of working because of him. But he couldn't have gotten a word out if he'd tried.

Susannah was beautiful.

For the last two weeks, he'd told himself she wasn't anywhere near as gorgeous as she was in his dreams. He'd concentrated on that first view he'd had of her, the jeans, the sneakers, the hair, the doughnut.

Now he knew he'd been kidding himself.

She was beautiful, and she'd been beautiful that morning, too, despite the jeans, the sneakers, the hair and the doughnut. For one wild instant, he thought of telling her so—and then he thought of her reaction if he swept her into his arms and said, "Miss Madison, you are one luscious-looking babe."

The thought made him smile, and when he smiled, the color heightened in her cheeks. Was that because he was still holding her hand? He hoped so.

He'd been too busy to stop in and see how she was doing these past weeks. Okay, he admitted to himself, he'd made sure he was too busy. It had been a business decision. He'd pumped money into *CHIC* and he wanted an even shot a recouping it, and instinct had told him the best way to do that was to give Susannah room. And she'd made it clear she needed space to get her job done.

Who was he kidding?

He'd kept away because he knew, if he was around her, his speech about sex being sex and business being business would turn into a joke. He wouldn't come onto her the way he had in the taxi. It would be a slow, sweet seduction this time, until she was breathless and hot and pleading with him to take her....

"My hand," she whispered.

Matthew blinked. "What?"

"You're hurting my hand."

He looked down. Her fingers had all but disappeared within his. The staff members had tried their best to disappear, too. People had drifted off into little clots, leaving them alone in a room full of surreptitious glances.

"Oh. Sorry." He released her hand, smiled politely. "Surprised to see me?"

"Very." Surprised? she thought. Stunned was closer to it. Her heart was tap-dancing, which was ridiculous. Her reaction to finding him here was ridiculous. The way he was looking at her was ridiculous, and there was only one way to handle it, and him. "In the future, please call and let me know you're coming."

Matthew's brows lifted. "Excuse me?"

"I said, I'd rather you didn't just drop in, Mr. Romano. Please telephone first and make an appointment."

"An appointment." The warm buzz was replaced by a cold sense of annoyance. He'd been standing here, thinking how good it was to see her again, and she'd been looking him up and down and feeling as pleased with his presence as a dog would with a colony of fleas. "An appointment, Miss Madison? Anybody would think you didn't want your publisher around."

Someone laughed nervously. Susannah shot a quick look around the room, and the place became silent.

"You have the right to disrupt the routine of this office anytime you please, of course."

"Disrupt?" Matthew said, very coldly.

Had she really said that? Susannah wrapped her arms around herself. "Ah, perhaps that's too strong a word to use."

"Not at all. Not if that's the word you want."

Matthew folded his arms. His jaw shot out. The air hummed with hostility, but it was too late to back off unless she wanted it to seem as if she were afraid of him.

"Very well, Mr. Romano." Susannah folded her arms, too, and tilted her chin. "It's exactly the word I want."

The indrawn gasps almost emptied the room of air.

"Uh, Suze?" Claire said hesitantly. "Mr. Romano, ah, Matthew, ah, Matt said—he said he was interested in hearing how the sexiest restaurant thingy was going, so we were, ah, we were telling him all about it, and—"

"If Mr. Romano has questions, he should ask them directly of me."

Matthew's mouth formed a smile that threatened to send the temperature plummeting.

"I did, Miss Madison. The other day, remember? I faxed and asked how the restaurant feature was coming along. Your reply indicated that it was coming along splendidly." That icy smile flickered across his lips again. "That was your word, wasn't it? 'Splendidly'?"

"Yes," she said, mentally crossing her fingers, "it was."

"You said you'd had many excellent suggestions, and that you'd narrowed them down to..."

"Six."

"Six. From which you'll select the winner."

"Yes. Mr. Romano, you know all of this. And really, we're very busy, so—"

"How will you do that, Miss Madison?"

"I beg your pardon?"

"How will you select the winner?"

Susannah laughed politely. "How would you think, Mr. Romano?"

"I don't know," he said, ever so politely. "That's why I'm asking you."

Susannah looked into that handsome, smug face. Was he trying to trap her into something? It seemed so, but what? And why?

"It's all spelled out in the rules. I'll visit all six finalists—"

"I've read the rules."

Susannah's mouth was dry. He knew. About the twenty-four-hour days. About the restaurants that were only open at night. About the impossibility of getting it all done on time...

How? Was he a mind reader, along with everything else?

"Yes," she said, with a little smile and a toss of her head, "I know. It's a tough job, but somebody's got to—"

"Unfortunately, it's starting to look as if you won't."

Susannah blinked. "Won't what?"

"Please, Miss Madison, don't play coy. You've got an article to write, an interview to do. When do you expect to fit in six evenings and six dinners? It's impossible."

"It isn't impossible," she said coldly, drawing herself up to her full five feet four inches, wishing like hell she'd known he was coming so she could have worn heels.

"But it is." His smile was smooth as satin and twice as slippery. "Especially since you haven't even visited one of them, have you?"

"How did you..." Susannah glared at her staff. No one would make eye contact.

"I know because it's my business to know," Matthew said, "because I'm the publisher of this magazine, and because some members of your staff, at least, understand the need to provide meaningful information when I request it."

Susannah slapped her hands on her hips. "I suppose that's a roundabout way of saying you came here to spy on me."

"Don't blame your inadequacy on your people, Miss Madison. I simply asked them how the project was going and they, unlike you, saw no need to lie."

"I did not lie, Mr. Romano! I never lie!"

"No?"

"No!"

"Then you won't mind telling me if you're going to be able to have the next issue ready on time."

"Of course it'll be ready."

"Complete with the much-touted, highly publicized sexiest restaurant feature?"

"Certainly," she said, lying through her teeth.

It didn't have to be a lie. He was right. It was time she admitted it to herself, if not to him. Time was running out. She couldn't work until nine and ten in the evenings, then go to dinner at the six restaurants that had made the finals.

But she didn't have to.

She didn't really have to visit them all. Well, she did. But not for an entire evening. She could pop in, take a look, even request a quick tour of the kitchen. She'd look at the pictures the photographer took, check her notes, then make a choice.

Oh, it was a brilliant plan! And it was flawless. What could go wrong when you were narrowing a field of six Rembrandts down to one?

"Absolutely, it will be ready," she said, and smiled. But Matthew smiled, too. The hair on the back of her neck rose. The trap was about to be sprung. She could tell.

"You're planning on selecting a winner without paying a personal visit, aren't you, Miss Madison?"

Susannah shoved her hands deep into the pockets of her khaki trousers.

"Certainly not. I made a promise to our readers, and I intend to keep it."

"I'm happy to hear it. And, of course, you won't cut any corners. You'll spend a couple of hours, savor a bottle of wine, a full meal..."

Susannah blinked. Perhaps he really was a mind reader.

"I don't see that as necessary," she said pleasantly. "The restaurants are all highly recommended."

"So was La Strada, " he said, his smile turning into something that would have done Peter proud.

She waited. He waited. Finally, she gave in.

"Are you going to explain what you mean, Mr. Romano?"

"Certainly, Miss Madison. La Strada's in San Francisco. It had a wonderful reputation until it changed hands. Now they couldn't fill the seats if they gave the food away."

"Yes, well, I suppose those things can happen, but—"

"If *CHIC* is going to give coverage to these restaurants, we'd better be damned sure they're what we claim they are. Wouldn't you agree?"

It was a good thing she'd tucked her hands away because they were shaking.

"It's not a problem." She spoke coolly. At least, she hoped it was coolly. "I'll just ask some selective questions of the owner..."

Matthew chuckled. To her chagrin, so did a couple of others.

"Let me be sure I understand this. You'll phone and you'll say, 'Hello, this is Susannah Madison, from *CHIC* magazine. We're trying to determine the sexiest restaurant for a big feature we're doing, and you're on our short list. This feature will bring you incredible amounts of business. And oh, by the way, how's the kitchen situation? The service? Have you fixed the rickety chairs? Replaced the frayed napery? And have you, by any chance, matched the silverware yet? Should we feel comfortable listing you as one of the most romantic restaurants in New York?'" Matthew's voice hardened. "Or should we tell people that they'd better prepare themselves for a night in the Ptomaine Palace?'" His eyes narrowed to slits. "Well, Miss Madison? Does that sound about right?"

No one moved. No one spoke. No one seemed to take a

breath. Not even Susannah, who knew he was right and hated him for it.

"Are you asking for my resignation?" she asked, finally.

Matthew's eyes widened. If she hadn't known better, she'd really have believed it was in total innocence.

"Of course not! Your staff and I agree that you've been working as hard as any one human being could. I'm here to offer my help."

"Your help," she said carefully. "And that would mean?"

Offering to check out the six finalists himself? Volunteering to take a series of beautiful blondes—and not dumb ones, because she knew him well enough now to suspect dumb women would bore him silly—out for six evenings of romantic suppers?

"My immediate authorization for you to put on extra staff. You need more hands here, Susannah, to free up your time."

"Thank you," she said, and meant it. "That would be wonderful."

"And I'll clear my calendar for the next six evenings." He grinned. "As you said, dining at all these romantic spots is going to be a tough job, but somebody's got to do it."

Her stomach knotted. She'd been right. Matthew and the Blonde of the Month, out every night, and all on her behalf.

"That's very generous, Mr. Romano."

"Matthew," he said soothingly.

"Matthew." Susannah tried for a smile. "I know how busy you must be."

"Yes, but I have a vested interest in seeing *CHIC* succeed."

"I know. But to put yourself out this way—"

"I think the best approach will be for us to begin immediately." He looked over her head. "Pam?"

"Yes, sir."

"Would you be please phone the first restaurant on the list and make reservations for—is eight o'clock a good time for you, Susannah?"

"Is eight o'clock..." Susannah's smile turned to a look of horror. "You mean—you mean, you want me to go to dinner with you?"

"Certainly." His expression was polite and very proper.

"You promised our readers you'd choose the winning restaurant yourself."

"I know I did, but..."

But what? Susannah was trapped, and by her own pledge.

CHAPTER SEVEN

SUSANNAH stood before the open door of her bedroom closet in her robe and counted to ten.

Ten didn't do it.

Twenty wouldn't, either.

Nothing, *nothing* would take the edge off her anger except a headline in the paper that said Matthew Romano had moved his business interests to Mars.

Oh, damn.

She groaned and flung herself on the bed. It was seven o'clock. She had half an hour to choose something to wear, fix her hair, put on her makeup. Half an hour before she had to carry out her sentence and have dinner with that obnoxious man.

"The nerve of the man, Peter," she said, "the nerve!"

"Mrrow." Peter leaped onto the bed and settled happily on her chest, paws kneading her terry-cloth robe in contentment.

Susannah sighed and stroked his silken fur.

"You cannot imagine how horrible he is, Petey. And how self-centered. Why, compared to Matthew Romano, you're the essence of humility."

"Mrrow?" Peter asked, and butted his head against Susannah's jaw.

"I know, I know, it seems impossible, but it's the truth. Actually, I'm amazed the city's big enough to hold him and his ego." An image of Matthew carting a blob-shaped ego flashed through her head, and she giggled. "Oh, how I'd love to tell him that. How I'd love to tell him to take his attitude and his magazine and tuck them both up his…"

The doorbell buzzed.

"Bankroll," she said, and sat up.

It was only ten minutes past the hour. Susannah's stomach clenched. Surely, Matthew wouldn't have arrived so early?

But he had. A glance through the peephole confirmed it.

She swung around and pressed her back to the door.

He couldn't come in. She'd specifically, explicitly told him she'd meet him downstairs, in the lobby. Actually, she'd told him she'd meet him at eight o'clock at Aunt Sally's, the first restaurant on the list.

"A Romantic Evening," he'd said, in that smarmy tone she hated, and in a way that made her see the capital letters that began both words, "does not begin with a man and woman arriving separately at their destination."

"We are not a man and woman," she'd said, "we are an editor and her publisher."

Matthew and everyone within hearing had laughed gaily, as if she'd made a charming joke, and then Matthew had said, most politely, that he'd be at her door at seven-thirty, and she'd said no, she'd meet him in the lobby.

The doorbell buzzed again. "Susannah?"

A muscle ticked in her jaw. Perhaps it was time to learn to count to ten in Urdu, she thought, and she turned, undid the locks and flung open the door.

"You're not supposed to be here yet, Mr. Romano."

Matthew grinned. "And good evening to you, too, Miss Madison.

"I said I'd meet you in the lobby. And you said you'd come by at—"

The tirade caught in her throat.

What a gorgeous sight he was. Aunt Sally's was very casual—the recommendations had all emphasized that—and casual was the way Matthew was dressed. He was standing in the doorway, smiling, wearing what looked like well-used hiking boots, faded jeans, a deep blue sweater and a leather jacket that looked as if its patina of age really came from hard use.

So what? Susannah thought, gathering her wits together. The only hard use the jacket would have seen would have been in its manufacture. Ditto for the boots. As for the man's good looks, there was no reason to gawk. His looks had never been in question. He was handsome, she was willing to admit that—assuming you liked the type.

"At seven-thirty," she said briskly. "And it's barely—"

"Seven-fifteen. I know. But the guy delivered my car earlier than I expected, and I couldn't see much sense in having the doorman park it for twenty minutes, so I drove over and there was a space right downstairs.''

"Your car?'' she asked blankly.

"Yeah. I rented one. I know everybody jokes about New York being the last place on earth to own an automobile, but heck, I'm a California product. A car's a part of life.'' He sighed at the look on her face. "Okay. I'm early, and I apologize. I'll sit down on that couch and I promise you won't even know I'm here.''

An apology was more than she'd expected. "Well, all right. Come in. I'll make you some coffee and you can drink it while I get—''

Dressed, she'd almost said. Such a simple word, but it made her suddenly aware of how she must look, in her old robe, her bare toes peeking out from under the hem.

Aware of how simple it would be to go to him, put her arms around his neck, lift her mouth to his for his kiss.

"On second thought,'' she said, "I'm all out of coffee.''

Matthew nodded. "No problem. I was only joking. You just go ahead, forget I'm here and get—''

Dressed.

That was the word. He knew she hadn't been able to say it, and damned if he could, either. Beneath the word, the truth lay shimmering like starlight on a field of snow. He didn't want Susannah dressed. He wanted her undressed, naked, in his arms. And despite all her indignation, all her protests, he knew it was what she wanted, too.

What would happen if he put an end to the lies? If he took her in his arms and kissed her? Opened the sash of that foolishly girlish robe, drew it away from her shoulders, buried his face in her throat and kissed his way down to her breasts?

Oh, hell.

He turned his back, put his hands into his pockets and marched to the window where he admired a truly spectacular view of a line of trash cans at the curb.

"Just get dressed,'' he said, his voice suddenly harsh. "I'm only a few minutes early, Madison. Common sense would have told you to be ready and waiting.''

So much for his apologies. The smile faded from Susannah's face.

"And common courtesy would have told you not to show up where you weren't invited."

She marched into the bedroom, slammed the door and scooped Peter from the bed where he waited.

"You were right not to come out," she said into his fur. "The man's an animal."

"Mrrow?" Peter said, in softest cat speak.

"Oh, not an animal like you, Petey darling. He's a beast. You know the Doberman down the hall? Believe me, the dog has a better personality than Matthew Romano."

Aunt Sally's was crowded, noisy and smoky.

It was, Matthew thought, about as romantic as an L.A. freeway at rush hour.

It was, Susannah thought, about as charming as a subway car at five o'clock.

She pulled a small notebook from her purse after they were seated.

"I made up a checklist."

Matthew's brows rose. "A checklist?"

"Uh-huh. There are five categories. Ambience. Décor. Food. Wine. Mood. And ratings from one to five."

"Ratings? You mean, stars?"

"I guess."

He put his elbow on the table and propped his chin in his hand. "Hearts," he said.

Susannah looked puzzled. "Hearts?"

"Sure. Little hearts. Instead of stars. One heart, two hearts, three…"

"Oh." She smiled. "Yes. Okay. That's a great idea."

He watched as she bent her head and scribbled in her notebook. "Just trying to be helpful," he said, and wondered if her hair felt as soft as he remembered.

"Anyway," she said, looking up, "I'm going to rate the restaurants on… Is something wrong?"

Matthew frowned and cleared his throat. "No, no. I, ah, I was only thinking… Ambience, you said. And décor and mood? But those are all the same thing."

Susannah gave him a pitying smile. "Not at all, Mr. Romano. Ambience is the overall feel of the place."

"The feel of it," he repeated.

She nodded. "Does it give off an aura of romance? Is it charming? Is it a place a couple would be likely to remember?"

Matthew looked around. The closest to an aura of anything was the overwhelming smell of charcoal drifting from the kitchen.

"And décor?"

"Décor is—well, it's décor. How the place is furnished, the table settings, whatever."

He nodded. They'd been seated at a table with one rickety leg, which he'd propped with a matchbook after his water glass had almost slid into his lap. The place mats listed the menu offerings, and two tines of his fork were bowlegged.

"Right. And mood?"

"Mood is the easiest one to judge. It's—"

Susannah clamped her mouth shut. How stupid not to have thought of revising the list once Romano had invited himself along.

"Mood," she said, trying to sound nonchalant, "mood is, ah, whether a dinner here would put a couple in the mood for, ah, for... You know."

Of course he knew. But he liked the fact that she was squirming under his gaze. Her cheeks were turning pink. Her throat, too. She was wearing a sweater with a vee neckline and he wondered, idly, just how far down her body that soft glow of color would stretch.

So he smiled pleasantly, linked his hands on the table and gave her a look that would have done a choirboy proud.

"No," he said blithely, "I don't. The mood for what?"

Was he dense? Or was he playing games at her expense? Either way, Susannah wasn't going to prolong the agony.

"Sex," she hissed, just as the waitress arrived to take their orders.

"I can come back later," she said, and winked.

Susannah turned a shade of crimson Matthew had never believed possible.

"We'll order now," she said.

And they did.

They drove back to her apartment in silence.

"A one for ambience," Matthew said.

Susannah nodded. "And for décor."

Matthew agreed. "The food was good, though," he said.

He figured it was good, anyway, considering the platters that had kept coming from the busy kitchen. But he'd been busy, too, watching Susannah delicately lift a rib to her mouth, nibble at it with even white teeth, then run the tip of her soft pink tongue around her lips, so busy that he'd hardly managed to choke down a bite.

"Yes," Susannah said, "it was."

It must have been. The couple at the next table had devoured a stack of ribs and a platter of chicken. She'd forced herself to eat one rib, but it hadn't been easy, watching Matthew lift a chicken leg to his mouth, watching his white teeth sink into the soft flesh.

"Five hearts for food," she said briskly, and scribbled in her notebook. "And the list of wine and beer was pretty thorough."

Matthew pulled his rented Porsche to the curb in front of her apartment building.

"That ale," he said, "the one from that microbrewery? It was excellent."

"Good." She made another note. Then she undid her seat belt, gave him a quick smile and reached for the door.

"I'll see you up."

"No! No, it isn't nec—"

But Matthew was already out of the car, opening her door and waiting for her to step out.

"This really isn't necessary," she said politely, as she stepped onto the sidewalk. "I'm perfectly capable of finding my own way upstairs."

"I'm sure you are." Matthew took her arm. "I know it's probably politically incorrect, but I don't believe in letting a woman go upstairs alone at night."

"Such an antiquated, machismo thing," Susannah said,

beaming at him as they quick-marched through the lobby. "I'm sure your dates must be terribly impressed."

"My DBs," he said, beaming right back at her as the elevator doors opened. "Isn't that what you meant to say?"

She lifted her chin. "If the shoe fits," she said, tossing her head.

They stood locked in silence until the doors opened. Then they walked to the door of her apartment.

"Key," Matthew said, holding out his hand.

Arguing, she suspected, would be useless. She dug in her purse, took out her keys, slapped them into his palm with all the delicacy of an operating room nurse handing over a scalpel. He put the key in the lock, turned it, opened the door an inch and handed the key to her.

"Good night, Susannah."

"Good night, Mr. Romano."

His teeth glittered in an icy smile.

"Try calling me Matthew. It's much more appropriate, considering the shock you gave our waitress tonight."

"Matthew," Susannah said, willing herself not to blush at the memory. "Thank you for a completely unnecessary evening."

He couldn't help it, that made him laugh. Even her lips twitched ever so slightly.

"You're welcome." He turned, took a couple of steps, then swung back and looked at her. "Your checklist," he said.

Susannah arched a brow. "What about it?"

"We did numbers one through four. We never got to number five."

She shrugged. "Mood? The answer's obvious, I think."

Matthew nodded. "It is," he said, and walked slowly toward her.

Susannah saw the look on his face. Her heart began to gallop.

"There can't be any debate about it," she said, far more calmly than she felt. "Aunt Sally's gets a broken heart for mood."

His mouth tilted in a smile that made her take a step back.

"I agree. If a man and woman were hoping for a place to

put them in the mood for sex, Aunt Sally's would never score."

"Matthew," Susannah said uneasily.

"Susannah," he said, and reached for her, and she went straight into his arms. They closed around her. She moaned, rose on her toes, linked her hands behind his head and sought his mouth. His teeth sank gently into her bottom lip. Her tongue caressed his. His hands swooped under her jacket, under her sweater, and cupped her breasts.

And, just when she thought her knees were going to buckle, he let her go.

"Tomorrow night," he said calmly. "Same time."

Susannah nodded. "Of course," she said, just as calmly.

She went into her apartment, shut the door, leaned against it and told herself that only an idiot would slide to the floor.

In the elevator, heading to the lobby, Matthew had a very similar conversation with himself.

The Gilded Carousel was supposed to be elegant.

Posh, the recommendations had said.

Do I look posh? Susannah wondered the next evening as she looked in the mirror.

She'd borrowed a calf-length beaded dress from a photo shoot. It was midnight blue shot with silver sequins and had a scooped neckline and long sleeves. She'd borrowed a pair of high heels, too. There hadn't been much choice, really. She had nothing even close to posh in her wardrobe, and she certainly wasn't going to go out and spend a small fortune on a dress she'd never use again.

A smile touched her mouth.

She wasn't sure about looking posh—whatever that meant—but she did look…

Pretty.

It wasn't a word she used very much, especially about herself. Her looks were fine. She didn't agonize over the fact that her hair curled too much on humid days, or that her mouth was just a bit too large, or that her skin tended to freckle if she spent too much time in the sun, and she was eternally grateful that she had thick, dark lashes, because that meant one less bit of makeup to have to bother using when she was in a rush.

Not that she'd dressed in a rush tonight. She'd taken a long bath instead of a shower, in a tub scented with lily of the valley bath oil. She'd brushed her hair dry so the curls were glossy. She'd splurged on lacy underwear because the dress called for it, certainly not for any other reason.

And the result was that she looked pretty.

Would Matthew notice?

Not that she wanted him to. It was only that a romantic evening—a real one, which this, surely, was not—would involve a man complimenting a woman on how she looked, wouldn't it?

Susannah stared at her reflection. A romantic evening, she thought.

The doorbell rang.

She frowned, glanced at the clock. She'd made it a point to be ready early. But Matthew was earlier still.

"Good evening," she said formally, when she opened the door—and tried not to let her mouth drop open, too.

If he'd been gorgeous last night, in jeans and a leather jacket, what word could possibly describe him tonight?

He was wearing a tux. A tux! The last time she'd gone out with a guy in a tux had been in high school, the night of her senior prom, and dear, sweet Sam had certainly not looked like this in his rented-for-the-occasion evening wear. His pants had been too short, his jacket sleeves too long, and his collar had tilted to the west.

Matthew's collar didn't tilt at all.

The tux fit as if it had been made for him—which, she had no doubt, it had. He looked—there was no other word—gorgeous.

The sexiest man alive, she thought, and a dangerous little hum of excitement danced through her blood.

"Hi." Matthew gave her a lazy smile. "I know I'm early," he said, and wondered if his nose would start growing for the lie. "I didn't mean to be, it just worked out that way."

Of course, he'd meant to be. He'd hoped to catch her in her robe again, or maybe even as she was coming out of the shower, when she'd have looked soft and flushed and...

"Beautiful," he said softly. "Susie, you are the most beautiful thing I've ever seen."

Susannah pinkened. "It's the dress."

"Like hell it is." He smiled. "Not that the dress isn't spectacular. Turn around so I can admire the view from all angles."

She laughed, blushed harder, but did as he asked.

"They said the restaurant was—"

"Posh." Matthew grinned and swept a hand the length of his jacket. "I know. That's the reason for the monkey suit."

"Don't apologize. You look…" Their eyes met. "You look…very nice."

"Thanks." He reached past her, took the silk coat she'd borrowed from Claire from the chair where she'd left it and draped it around her shoulders. His hands drifted across the nape of her neck, lingering for no more than a second.

A tremor went through her.

"Cold?"

Susannah smiled brightly and picked up her small silver evening bag. "No, no, I'm fine. Just a—"

"A goose walking across your grave." He grinned again. "My grandmother says stuff like that. Doesn't yours?"

"My grandmother?" Susannah thought of her prim New England grandmother, a woman who'd refused to admit anyone existed unless they could trace their ancestry to the *Mayflower,* and never mind that the Madison family had been dead broke for years and years, and she laughed. "My grandmother—the only one I ever knew, anyway—would probably have fainted if anyone ever said anything so earthy around her."

"Ah," he said, "well, Nonna is Sicilian. She's earthy, all right."

"Sicilian?" Susannah asked, looking at him. "Really?"

"Oh, yeah. She came to this country when she was twelve, but you'd never know it." The boyish grin spread over his face again. "She used to whack me across the backside whenever she figured I needed it, but I loved her anyway. And she made the most incredible lasagna. We had dinner at her house every Sunday when I was a kid. It was my father's one day off, and we used to put on our good clothes, go to church, then go to Nonna's for dinner. She lived right around the corner from us, in North Beach."

"North Beach in San Francisco?" She couldn't keep the surprise from her voice. "Isn't that—"

"Little Italy. They still call it that, I guess." Matthew opened the door and Susannah stepped past him into the hall. "All I know is, if the guys I grew up with saw me in this outfit, I'd end up having to defend my honor."

She laughed, and he laughed, but her head was spinning. Matthew Romano, born in one of San Francisco's old ethnic neighborhoods?

So, maybe he hadn't spent his life just sitting around and counting his money, after all.

The Gilded Carousel looked as if it might be the real thing.

"Posh isn't even the word," Susannah whispered over a flute of Dom Pérignon.

"Uh-huh. I keep thinking they're going to ask to see our pedigrees."

"My grandmother—remember her?"

"Certainly. The old broad with the fancy ancestors."

Susannah laughed. "That's her. She'd be happy to oblige."

"Well, hell, Susie, why not?" Matthew smiled. "I'm impressed. A gen-u-ine descendent of *Mayflower* stock is nothing to sneeze at."

"Trust me, Matthew, it's meaningless. I grew up in a big, run-down house on Beacon Hill."

"Boston?"

"Uh-huh. And I grew up hearing all about the Daughters of the American Revolution and the Founding Fathers—and pretending that, when the lights suddenly went out, it was because of a power failure, not because the electric bill hadn't been paid."

Susannah straightened in the gilded, elegant chair. Why on earth had she said that? She never talked about her childhood. Never. What was the point? Life was what you made of it, and she'd been working like a demon to make the most of hers as long as she could remember.

"Sorry," she said, forcing a smile to her lips. "There's no reason to bore you with my family history."

"I'm not bored at all. Actually, I'm amazed that the *Mayflower* crowd has the same problems as the bunch from Little Italy."

"Not all of it." Susannah waited while the waiter served her shrimp scampi and Matthew's boeuf en croute. "Some of them have money. And some of the ones that don't aren't embarrassed to go out and earn it."

"But not Grandma?"

Susannah pretended to be shocked. "Grandmother, if you please. No, not her. One didn't discuss finances. It was…lower class."

"In other words, it was better to pretend there'd been a power failure than to admit you couldn't pay the electric bill," Matthew said, and smiled.

"Exactly. My father agreed. Or didn't want to quarrel with her. Whatever. He had no real skills, so he toyed with selling stocks and insurance to people he knew—people who, I suppose, felt sorry for him—but when he died, we were really broke. The house went for taxes. My mother went to work. She got a job as a saleswoman in—" she smiled "—in a posh little shop where she spent her time waiting on people who'd once pretended to be her friends."

Matthew's smile disappeared. "It sounds like a rough childhood," he said, his eyes fixed on her face.

"No. Oh, no. I know that lots of people have it much worse. And, in a way, I suppose it was a good lesson."

He reached across the table, his hand curling around hers.

"In making sure the electric bill gets paid?" he asked, smiling a little.

Susannah laughed. "Yes. And in the importance of being able to make my own way in this world." His hand felt wonderful, holding hers. Hard. Warm. Protective. Carefully, she disengaged her fingers and sat back. "Don't look at me that way, Matthew. Really, I know it's silly to complain about having grown up pretending to be rich. I mean, we always had food on the table and a roof over our heads. Lots of people have less." She picked up her fork and stabbed a shrimp. "Anyway, that's all in the past. Grandmother died years ago, and my mother lives in an apartment. She's got a job she likes, and friends…''

Suddenly, she seemed to hear the endless prattle of her own voice. The fork dropped from her hand to the table. She dipped her head, made more out of recovering it than it was worth. When she looked up, her expression was composed and serene.

"We might have to score the Gilded Carousel a broken heart for ambience," she said lightly. "Any place that makes me cough up the family secrets couldn't possibly have ambience. My grandmother would tell you that."

Matthew nodded. She wanted to change the subject. Well, that was fine. This entire conversation was making him uneasy. Not the things Susannah had told him about herself. He wanted to know more about her, and he'd been completely caught up in listening to her and in watching the play of emotion on her lovely face.

The uneasiness came from something else entirely.

Seconds ago, for no good reason, he'd suddenly found himself thinking how much his nonna and Susannah would like each other.

It was such a pointless thought that it had made everything around him blur.

Now he was thinking something even more pointless.

He'd sat opposite scores of beautiful women in his life, half listening as they babbled about everything from parties to politics. He knew how to look interested and how to say all the right things, but he couldn't, for the life of him, recall ever wanting to take a woman into his arms and tell her—and tell her…

The hair rose on the back of his neck.

Carefully, very carefully, Matthew put down his fork and his knife.

"I hope you don't mind," he said politely, "but I'm afraid we're going to have to pass on coffee and dessert."

Susannah looked up. Heat swept through her veins.

She had embarrassed him. Embarrassed herself. She could see it in his face. His smile was polite, his eyes cool, and she knew that he was counting the minutes until he could end the evening.

Whatever had possessed her to tell him the silly story of her life? Matthew Romano was her boss. He was a man who'd tried to seduce her. His interest in her began in the office and ended in bed, and since she'd made it clear she wouldn't be making any stops there, that was the end of it.

Why had she bored him with all her very private baggage?

She knew better than to make things worse by apologizing. Instead, she pasted a bright smile to her lips, folded her napkin and dropped it beside her plate.

"Mind? Matthew, that's perfect. I was going to suggest the same thing." She tried not to think about how quickly he rose from his seat or how, when he helped her with her coat, there was no lingering brush of his hand against her neck. "I have an early meeting tomorrow. You know how it is."

He didn't. He didn't know how anything was, not at this moment, but he wasn't going to admit that to her or to himself.

"I do, indeed," he said pleasantly. "In fact, I have a meeting, too. In Los Angeles." He took her elbow as they left the restaurant and walked to his car. "I meant to mention it, Susannah. I might not be back for a while."

"Oh." She swallowed her disappointment. "Well, that's no problem. It really wouldn't be so awful if I checked out the other restaurants—" alone, she'd been going to say, but the word stuck in her throat "—if I checked them out with someone not connected to *CHIC*."

He swung toward her, his face suddenly harsh in the lamplight.

"Peter?" he said.

Peter? she thought. *Peter?* And then she remembered.

"Peter, yes," she said, and smiled brilliantly. "He's—he's really got excellent taste in—in fine dining. I'm sure he'd—" Her words died away. They stood looking at each other. *Tell me you don't want me to go out with Peter,* Susannah thought suddenly, *say it...*

"Or Sam," Matthew said, with a glittering smile.

"Well, no. Sam's on—"

"Cape Cod. With Mama." A muscle danced in his cheek. He took her arm and hurried her toward his Porsche, unlocked the door and motioned her inside. "Take anyone you want," he said. "It doesn't matter."

Twenty minutes later, after they'd said a polite good-night, Susannah stood inside her dark apartment.

"It doesn't matter to me, either," she said into the silence.

She'd check out the rest of the restaurants alone. Matthew was wrong. She didn't need him with her. No more evenings wasted, no more senseless small talk...

Something silky and soft wound gently around her ankles.

"Mrrow?" said Peter.

Susannah smiled and scooped the cat into her arms.

"Why on earth would it matter?" she said.

And then, for no reason whatsoever, she buried her face in Peter's fur and wept.

CHAPTER EIGHT

IT WAS late in the day, and the *CHIC* team was gathered in the boardroom for a brainstorming session.

They sat around a conference table heaped with photos, notepads and computer printouts. A coffee urn, packets of artificial sweetener and an open jar of powdered creamer stood on the sideboard, flanked by half-empty boxes of rapidly aging bagels and pastries from Doughnuts Deelishus.

People, deep in thought, sat tilted back in their chairs, slumped over the table or staring into space, waiting for that elusive killer of an idea to spring into their brains.

Susannah's brain, unfortunately, seemed to have died. As far as she could tell, there wasn't a clever idea in it.

She reached for her coffee, then hesitated. Maybe the problem was too much artificial sweetener. Or too much caffeine. Wasn't it caffeine that was supposed to give cancer to laboratory rats? She couldn't remember. She couldn't remember much of anything, not after the last couple of weeks.

Everybody at *CHIC* was exhausted.

The world's sexiest restaurant issue had just hit the stands, and it was a smash hit. The distributors said they couldn't stock shelves fast enough to meet the demand, and advertising space was being sold at a premium for the next issue. But if they didn't capitalize on their momentum by making that next issue bigger and better, *CHIC* would slide right back downhill.

The hot-button feature for the next issue—the world's sexiest getaway—was ready to go. The editorial staff had chosen three incredible places. They'd photographed all of them, and now they were ready to declare one the winner, with an extra-special photo spread to be shot on its romantic premises.

And that would take them to the February issue. The sexiest man alive.

What had started almost as a gag had turned into the feature of the year. Distributors, readers, newspaper columns, even TV shows, were giving the sexiest man terrific publicity.

CHIC, of course, was doing more than its part.

"Just wait until you see us for Valentine's Day," the current magazine gushed, "when we'll bring you The Sexiest Man Alive. Yummy! You'll drown in his gorgeous eyes, meet him up close and personal, complete with a no-holds-barred, pull-out centerfold."

The copy made Susannah groan, but she knew it would sell lots of magazines. Actually, it already had. Readers had sent in nominations by the carload, and Susannah's staff had narrowed the list to four finalists.

Bart Fitt, whose bare buns of gold had given new meaning to the words *camera close-ups* on a highly rated, late-night TV soap.

Alejandro Rio, the handsome male model for Cotton Puffs underwear, whose glorious male assets bulged in the briefest pair of briefs on a billboard above Times Square.

Zeke McCool, the smoky-voiced lead singer for a hot new band, who pranced around onstage with his shirt off so that his impressive abs had millions of women begging to do his laundry.

And Stefan Zyblos, a writer with a whiskey voice and a steamy smile, whose highly anticipated first novel was said to be so erotic it was going to be sold with oven mitts.

"Something for everyone," Claire had sighed, after a day spent narrowing the choices, "and, by golly, studly to the bone."

Susannah had smiled in agreement and wished she'd never used the silly word.

"But no studlier than our Mr. Romano," Claire had added, with a quick look at Susannah, who'd pretended not to hear.

Why would she? She didn't think about Matthew anymore. Not in any way that mattered. Not so that she felt the foolish, almost overwhelming sadness she'd felt the night he'd walked out of her life, or the days and the nights after.

Susannah frowned, let her chair fall forward so that the legs hit hard against the floor and went to get another doughnut. It tasted like cardboard, but she chewed and swallowed methodically until she'd finished the last crumb. Then she licked the powdered sugar from her fingertips.

Artificial sweeteners, caffeine, sugar be damned.

So what if she was on chemical overload? She had work to do and she needed the energy. That her thoughts had drifted off the subject and onto a dead issue like Matthew only proved it. He'd disappeared as soon as he'd decided that bedding her wasn't a prize worth pursuing, and a day didn't go by that she didn't breathe a sigh of relief. She had nothing at all to do with him. Joe Romano was her contact now. When she needed an okay for something that crept beyond her budget, he was the man she got in touch with.

Joe was easy to deal with. Helpful, too. He loved the sexiest getaway and the sexiest man stuff. In fact, he'd been the one who'd suggested they feature all four of the sexiest man finalists in the Valentine's Day issue, not just the winner.

"Pose the winning guy in nothing but a jockstrap," Joe had E-mailed, "and we'll sell out in an hour."

Susannah thought he was probably right. The issue wasn't shaping up as she'd imagined it—sex was battling it out with romantic, and sex was winning—but hey, that's how it was in real life, too. Just look at what had happened with Matthew. A romantic evening, her in a gown, him in a tux, a romantic restaurant, and what had happened? She'd revealed more of herself than she should have, that was what, and it had scared him off.

And a good thing, too. Who wanted somebody like that hanging around?

Why was she wasting time thinking about him? Matthew was the past. *CHIC*'s February issue was the future—assuming she ever managed to get it on the stands.

Not so long ago, she and her staff had been short on ideas. Now what they needed was time. Time to cover the sexiest getaways, pick a winner, send a team to photograph it. Time to interview the sexiest man finalists. Time to choose one guy as the sexiest man alive, to arrange for the centerfold shot. Time to make the next two issues absolute winners.

Time, she thought, and sighed.

She'd sent out a memo called Solving Our Logistics

Problem, and now here they were, her entire staff, pigging out on doughnuts, overdosing on coffee...and getting nowhere.

"It's impossible," Marcy from marketing said as she reached for her umpteenth cup of coffee.

"Impossible," Amy from fashion agreed, and bit into a buttered bagel.

"Impossible or not," Susannah said, trying to sound upbeat and perky, "we have to find a way to deliver."

"Absolutely," Marcy said.

The room feel silent.

"We could always chain the sexiest finalists to our desks," Amy said.

There was a ripple of halfhearted laughter.

"Or ship them off for a weekend at the getaway finalists," Marcy said. "The old two birds with one stone thing."

Another ripple of laughter rang hollow in the room.

"There's got to be a solution," Claire said. "We just haven't thought of it yet."

Susannah nodded along with all the others. She trusted her team. They were sharp. She'd learned to let them brainstorm and to stay out of the early discussions as much as possible.

"Plus another great cover," Amy said, "every bit as hot as the current one."

There was a murmur of agreement. Susannah sighed, leaned her arms on the table and cradled her head. Her gaze drifted past Amy to the huge blowup of the December cover, which hung on the boardroom wall.

It was an interior shot of the Gilded Carousel. Candles, snowy-white napery, glittering wine goblets and a sexy couple from the modeling agency gazing into each other's eyes across a platter of hors d'oeuvres.

"Oh, sexy," Claire had sighed when she'd seen the proofs from the shoot. "That guy's probably thinking about his boyfriend, but from here, he looks as if he's ready to grab her hand and leap into bed."

"You think it'll sell?" Susannah had asked.

"Like crazy. Although they could just as well have taken a shot of you and our sexy publisher. Now, there's a man who wouldn't have any trouble getting me to jump between the sheets."

Susannah had busied herself with arranging the proofs into a neat stack.

"That's because you didn't have to sit across a table from him, pretending you were having a good time."

"Pretending? How could a woman not have a good time, out on a dinner date with that gorgeous hunk?"

"He did not take me on a date. He accompanied me on assignments for the magazine. And I don't really see why you'd call him a gorgeous hunk."

"Wrong adjective? Sorry. A studly hunk." Claire had grinned. "Come on, Suze, you can't deny that just thinking about the guy is a turn-on."

"For you, maybe," Susannah had said, with a smile that said she was above such foolishness. "I don't think of him at all."

It was, of course, a lie.

"Suze?"

Susannah blinked and sat up straight. Everybody was looking at her, their expressions expectant.

"Suze? You agree that it sounds good?"

People were smiling and nodding. Well, what the heck. Susannah smiled and nodded, too. Then she picked up her pencil, pulled a notepad toward her and made what she hoped were convincing doodles on the page.

She did think about Matthew. A lot. And the more she did, the more angry she became.

All that stuff about staying in New York to oversee the magazine had been nonsense. He'd never given a damn about *CHIC*. Why would he? Its failure would be a dent in the Romano empire. Its success would be a barely noticeable blip.

The truth was that he'd stayed so he could set things up for what she thought of now as the Big Seduction Scene.

And wasn't it just too bad she'd spoiled it? First she'd told him something about herself, when anyone could see that he was not a man interested in exchanging cozy confidences with whatever woman he'd set his sights on. She'd sensed that from the first day she saw him on Cape Cod with a blonde. What he wanted was sex, the same as all *CHIC*'s readers, busily plunking down their two ninety-eight for the current issue. Not that there was anything wrong with wanting sex. It was just that her interests were elsewhere. She didn't need them diverted from the one meaningful goal...

Success.

Susannah sighed and worked the tip of the pencil across the page.

No, she certainly hadn't wanted any involvement with Matthew. Still, it was a good thing for her pride that she'd let him think there was already a man in her life and in her bed. A man named Peter.

Peter...Katz.

Susannah's lips twitched. How come she'd never thought of it before? Peter Katz, her companion in bed. Peter Katz, sitting across from her at the kitchen table, wearing a tux.

She laughed, and Claire let out a shriek that almost started Susannah out of her skin.

"You like it," Claire said. "Oh, wow, Suze, you like it!"

"What?" Susannah asked, staring at the smiling faces around the table while her heartbeat fell back toward normal.

Claire looked at everybody one by one. "Be honest, guys. Didn't you all think we were going to have to push this one on our fearless leader?"

Heads nodded in eager agreement. Susannah felt a tingle of alarm. What were they all excited about? What had she just implied she was excited about, too?

"I wasn't sure how you'd react, you know, Suze? After all, it's a little bit—"

"Crazy," Amy said, and giggled.

"Right," Claire said, "crazy, and probably expensive as heck—well, not when you realize all the incredible benefits."

Susannah looked around. Head bobbing seemed to have become the action of the hour.

"And the time problem," Marcy chirped. "The logistics thing. All taken care of, right?"

"Well," Susannah said, "well..."

"Nobody's ever done this before," Amy said. "You agree, Suze?"

Claire laughed as she looked at Susannah's face. "She's having second thoughts. You are, aren't you, Suze?"

"No. I mean, well, maybe. I mean..."

"I know. You're worried the Romanos won't approve."

"The Romanos," Susannah said, feeling like the only person at a party who didn't know the secret sign. "Yes, well—"

"Joe will go for it. It's a bundle of money, but he'll see that it's going to be well spent." Claire frowned. "Will he have to get Matthew's approval, do you think?"

Susannah cleared her throat. "I don't—actually, I don't think we—"

"That's true. If he needs Matthew's approval, it's Joe's problem, not ours. Although I can't imagine Matthew would give us the thumbs-down, either. How will you pitch it, Suze?"

Everyone looked at Susannah, who cleared her throat again.

"Tell you what, Claire. Since it's, ah, your plan, and you know the details better than any of us, why don't you try pitching it to me?"

Claire wrinkled her brow. "I just did."

"Oh, of course you did." Susannah laughed so gaily that she could almost see the *Ha, ha, ha's* spilling from her lips. "What I meant was, why don't you try pitching it as if you were me pitching it to Joe Romano? It would be a huge help."

Claire nodded, shut her eyes, took a deep breath, then looked at Susannah. "Mr. Romano," she said.

Everyone smiled.

"Mr. Romano, here's what we want to do." Claire pushed back her chair and got to her feet. "We've had enormous success with the current *CHIC* issue, and it's vital we stay on a roll." She stepped behind her chair, curled her hands around its top rung and looked seriously at Susannah. "This is our proposal, sir. We've narrowed our choice of sexiest getaways to one."

Susannah blinked. "We have?"

"Yes," Claire said impatiently, "remember? That's part of the plan. Eliminate that hotel in the Pocono Mountains, the lodge on Lake Michigan, the island in Seattle. They're all great, but they can't compare to Paris."

"Paris?" Susannah asked, sitting bolt upright. "As in Paris, France? I didn't even know we had a Paris contender."

"We didn't. I mean, we did. I mean, when you first told us about the sexiest getaway, you mentioned a weekend in Paris for a prize. "

"Yes, but I still don't remember anybody nominating a place in—"

"It was Amy's idea."

Amy smiled modestly. "Jimmy and I went there on our honeymoon." She blushed. "We had a suite in this hotel—"

"We send you to that hotel, Suze, " Claire said, while Amy sat back and sighed. "Along with a photographer, a makeup guy, a stylist…the works."

"Me?" Susannah's voice squeaked. "What for?"

"So we can photograph you," Claire said. "Honestly, Suze, weren't you paying attention?"

"I, ah, I must have misunderstood. Claire, this is silly. Photograph me? Why would our readers want to see—"

"Because," Claire said, as if she were explaining things to a somewhat backward five-year-old, "because, Suze, you are their personalized connection to *CHIC,* and to the life-style *CHIC* stands for, remember? That was your idea."

"Yes. Well, sure, but—"

"Well, what could be more personal, more romantic, more sexy, than Susannah Madison in Paris?"

"You're kidding.

"Susannah," half a dozen voices said, all of them fraught with exasperation.

"Susannah," Claire said, shaking her head, "you haven't been listening. Didn't I say this was an incredible idea? That it would save time? That it would make history?"

"Claire, *you* haven't been listening. There's nothing time-saving about photographing me in a Paris hotel, and the only thing incredible about it would be all our readers, shaking their heads and saying, well, there she is, a woman spending a weekend all by herself in the world's most romantic—"

"The world's sexiest—"

"The world's sexiest city," Susannah said, nodding at the Greek chorus that corrected her. She sat back, folded her arms and looked at Claire. "Right?"

Claire folded her arms and looked back. "Not all by herself," she said smugly. "You'll be in that suite with four, count 'em, four gorgeous studs."

Susannah blinked. "I beg your pardon?"

"We send you to Paris," Marcy said excitedly, "with our

sexiest guys. They wine you. They dine you. They take you dancing. You pose in the arms of every last one. You interview them. And Jimmy gets the pictures he needs for the getaway issue *and* for the Valentine's Day issue at the same time, with January leading straight into February. Ta da, we end up in the winner's circle.''

"Yes!'' Amy cried, and Claire edged forward in her chair. "Suze, what do you say?''

The room was silent, so silent Susannah could hear the cooing of the pigeons that spent their days on the ledge outside the window.

"Me?'' she said finally, "in Paris, with the sexiest men alive?''

She got to her feet, walked to the window and looked out. The pigeons were out there, all right. The big gray male with the iridescent neck feathers was all puffed up, as usual, strutting his stuff for the female. But she was making pigeon eyes at another bird, a handsome guy with silver on the tips of his wings.

The studly pigeon most certainly did not look happy.

Susannah swung around and smiled at her expectant staff.

"I think it sounds wonderful,'' she said, and the room rang with cheers.

Three thousand miles away, Matthew sat at the head of a glass-topped conference table, doing his best to concentrate on the presentations of his team of advisers.

There were four of them, including Joe. They were all people whose opinions he valued, whose advice he trusted, whose summaries he always treated with interest and respect.

Unfortunately, he hadn't heard a word any of them had uttered this morning.

Matthew's gaze went to the papers neatly stacked in front of his brother. There were notes. A file folder. A computer printout.

And that magazine. That ridiculous magazine. The current issue of *CHIC*.

His expression darkened. He couldn't see the entire cover, but he didn't have to. What he could see was enough. Who had approved it? Who had designed it? The photograph was terrible. What jerk had decided that a man would risk dipping his tie into his bouillabaisse to lean across a sea of white linen and gaze longingly into the eyes of a woman who looked as if what she needed most was not him but the food before her?

His mouth twisted with derision.

Women weren't supposed to be skinny creatures of skin and bone, they were supposed to be soft and curvy. Like—

The furrow between his brows deepened.

And that dress she was wearing. What man would have that besotted look in his eyes if his woman wore something that looked more like a skimpy nightgown than a dress? Something flowing and feminine could be a lot more sexy. He hadn't always thought so, but he'd changed his mind not long ago. A woman could stir a man's blood if she wore a dress shot with silver stars, a dress that lovingly defined the sweet, sweet curves of—

"Matt?"

He looked up. Joe was leaning toward him.

"Yes?"

"Frank wondered if you had any questions."

Matthew shot a look at his chief accountant. Frank looked like a puppy waiting for a pat on the head.

"Ah, no. No questions, Frank. Your report said it all."

Frank beamed. "Glad to hear it, Matt."

There was a silence, and Joe cleared his throat. "Did you want Beverly to pick up from here, Matt?"

"Beverly. Yes, yes, fine. That's an excellent idea."

Matthew pasted an attentive look on his face as his head of sales launched into her presentation. For some reason, he was having a tough time keeping his thoughts from wandering.

It was that magazine. That nonsensical magazine. Why wouldn't he keep thinking about it? After all, he'd tied up a considerable amount of money in its success or failure. Failure, for sure, considering the way this much-ballyhooed new cover looked.

Matthew put a fingertip on the edge of the magazine and eased it toward him.

Awful. Truly awful. The photo didn't capture the feel of the feature at all. For all he knew, it hadn't even been photographed inside the Gilded Carousel. Did the tables really look like that? Were the candles so tall? He didn't think so. Well, maybe he couldn't recall. The restaurant hadn't made much of an impression, and what did that tell him? That *CHIC* had been mistaken in selecting it. It hadn't been memorable at all. If it were, he'd know what the place looked like.

As it was, he could only remember Susannah. Susannah, with her cap of curls. Her pink mouth. Her way of melting into him, whenever he'd taken her in his arms...

Matthew pushed back his chair. It squeaked loudly against the polished parquet floor, and his vice president for new projects, who'd started to talk as soon as Beverly finished, looked up, surprised, and peered over his reading glasses.

"Sorry," Matthew said briskly, as he stood up, "but I'm going to have to cut this short."

Not even Joe could keep from looking startled. The little group rose to its feet. Matthew smiled pleasantly, shook hands all around, walked his people to the door. One by one, they filed out. Only his brother lingered. When the room was empty, he looked at Matthew.

"Something wrong?"

"No. Of course not." Matthew walked across the room to the serving table laid with a silver coffee service and half a dozen Spode cups and saucers. "Why should something be wrong? I just figured I'd heard enough for this morning." He poured coffee into a cup, added a dollop of cream and sipped the steaming brew. "You know Sorenson. He's a good man, but he never knows when to stop talking."

"Yeah. Especially when he's only gotten his opening sentence out of his mouth."

Matthew looked around. "Did I cut him off that fast?"

Joe grinned. "Faster than a speeding bullet."

"Oh." Matthew sighed, set his coffee down and walked to the window. The view was one of the reasons he'd bought this building for his headquarters. He could see clear to the Golden Gate Bridge and to the ocean beyond. "You think I was rude?"

"I think there's a little knot of people heading back to their offices, wondering if the roof's about to fall in on their heads."

Matthew sighed again. "You're probably right. Send them

a memo over my name. Tell them that today's reports
were—''

"Invaluable?" Joe said, straight-faced.

Matthew chuckled. "Let's not go overboard, okay? Tell
them their reports were very useful, that I'll take everything
they said under consideration, blah, blah, blah, and that I'm
looking forward to meeting with them again, as per schedule."

"Uh-huh." Joe nodded. "Just in time for Valentine's Day."

Matthew's eyes narrowed. "What's that supposed to
mean?"

"Hey, what could it mean? Just in time for Valentine's Day.
That's all."

"Yeah," Matthew said, after a minute. He turned his back
to the room and stared out the window. "I saw you have a
copy of *CHIC*."

"Uh-huh. It hit the stands today, but Susie—"

"Susannah."

"Sure," Joe said lazily. "Susannah. She sent me an ad-
vance copy, wanted to know what I thought."

"And?"

"And it's great. I E-mailed her right away and told her so."

"Great?" Matthew said, as if the word had a bad taste. He
looked at his brother. "That—that piece of sleaze is great?"

Joe's brows shot toward his hairline.

"Sleaze? *CHIC* magazine? Maybe if you've been living in
Shangri-La, but—"

"So it's not sleaze. That doesn't mean it has—it has…"

"Redeeming social values?" Joe snorted. "Damn right, it
hasn't. *CHIC* is fun. It's lighthearted. It's for a woman to relax
with at the end of a long day."

"Be sure and bill that description to the advertising
budget."

Joe snatched the copy of *CHIC* from the table. "Take a
look at what Susie—Susannah's—put together before you
knock it. The month before she took over, the cover showed
a woman knitting an afghan. This month—"

"I've seen it," Matthew said coolly. "You don't have to
wave it under my nose." Matthew strode across the room and
refilled his coffee cup. "Who chose those models? The
woman, especially."

His brother looked at the magazine. A smile curled his mouth. "I don't know. Some guy with good taste in babes, that's for sure."

"Taste?" Matthew sipped his coffee, grimaced and put the cup down. "The cover looks like a promo for bulimia. Just look at that woman, Joe. Skinny. Bony. And, as if that weren't enough, she's got an empty smile, a head full of bleached hair that looks as if it's been sprayed into place with Krazy Glue..."

Joe stuck his hands into his trouser pockets and rocked on his heels.

"On the other hand," he said lazily, "she's a dead ringer for the last six or seven broads you've dated."

Matthew's head jerked. "Are you nuts? I never go out with—" He glared at Joe, then at the magazine, and folded his arms over his chest. "I'll expect a better cover shot for the January issue," he said coldly.

Joe shrugged. "Whatever you say, boss."

Whistling softly through his teeth, the younger Romano brother strolled from the office.

Two nights later, Matthew had put *CHIC*, and Susannah, completely out of his thoughts.

He was having drinks with Phoebe Anson, who was, according to rumor, his latest interest. Phoebe was a model who hoped for a career as an actress. She was slender, blond and stunning. Or she was skinny, made-up within an inch of her life and about as real as a doll.

Matthew was having a difficult time deciding which. He was having a difficult time carrying his end of the conversation, too.

Phoebe was telling him about a commercial she'd auditioned for.

"It's this cute little character called Emmy? Emmy the Elf? Who lives under your sink? If you buy Elf-Bright detergent?"

Matthew nodded, told himself that the way her voice rose at the end of each sentence wasn't a pain in the butt but an adorable affectation and told himself, as well, that it wouldn't be polite to tell Phoebe the strip of phony lashes on her right eyelid was starting to come undone.

"My agent said it might be a problem? That I don't have average looks? So I thought about it and I just, you know, twisted my face a little? During my audition?"

Eyelashes weren't everything. Neither were perpetual question marks. Phoebe really was beautiful, if you liked the type. Which he did. Why wouldn't he? And she was fun. She was easygoing. He'd give her two and a half, no, three hearts....

What was he doing? He wasn't a judge at a beauty pageant. This mental score sheet thing was becoming ridiculous. He'd been doing it ever since he'd last seen—ever since he'd left New York. Date a woman, check off her attributes, do a quick comparison between her and—

Definitely ridiculous.

Any man in his right mind would have given tens to the last three women he'd dated, but he'd sat across from them, just the way he was sitting across from Phoebe, coldly, methodically picking them apart.

Was it him? Was he getting jaundiced at the age of thirty? Or was it the women? Were they becoming less desirable?

Matthew's lips twitched. Damn if he hadn't caught Phoebe's disease. He was thinking in question marks.

Who was he kidding?

He was thinking of Susannah.

That was the reason he couldn't seem to concentrate on any one woman or find one whose company he enjoyed. They were all gorgeous and fun to be with, and some of them could even carry on a conversation. But not one of them was Susannah.

Susannah, who'd argue about anything at the drop of a syllable.

Susannah, who could make a sweatshirt and jeans look sexy.

Susannah, who didn't need false eyelashes and a palette of paint to be beautiful.

Susannah, who could never have kissed a guy named Sam or one named Peter the way she'd kissed him, or they'd never have let her out of their arms.

"Matthew? I think that's your phone ringing?"

Matthew blinked. Phoebe was smiling prettily, head cocked, chocolate eyes big and round. She was right. His phone was making urgent sounds. He smiled back, apologized for the interruption and reached into his pocket.

It was Joe.

"Am I interrupting anything that shouldn't be interrupted?" he asked slyly.

Matthew looked at Phoebe. She took the cherry from her drink and gently rolled it between her lips.

"Not yet, you aren't. What's up?"

Joe's tone turned businesslike. "I figured you'd want to know the deal in Connecticut went through."

"Great. Anything else?"

"No, not really. Well, yeah. Something came in from New York a couple of days ago I think you might want to know about."

Matthew sighed. "Better late than never, right? What was it?"

"Susannah called and asked me to approve a chunk of money."

Phoebe, still playing games with the cherry, batted her lashes.

"How much did she ask for ?"

Joe named a sum. Matthew whistled.

"She planning on buying a small country?" he said, and smiled at Phoebe, who smiled back.

"Well, it seems she's got this hot idea…"

Matthew listened. And listened. When he figured he couldn't listen anymore, not without exploding, he mouthed an apology to Phoebe, who'd opened her compact to repair any ravages left by her exercise with the cherry, rose from the table and walked to the bar.

"Let me be sure I've got this right," he said slowly. "Susannah is going to Paris with a photographer, a makeup guy, a stylist, a hairdresser and a writer."

"More or less. There's a couple of others, too."

"They're going to stay in two-thousand-dollar-a-day suites—"

"Susie stays in the suite. Everybody else gets regular rooms."

"An admirable economy," Matthew said icily.

"Well, not everybody else. Stefan, Bart, Zeke and Alejandro get suites, too. But you'd figure that."

The Four Stooges? Matthew thought wildly.

"Who?" he asked.

"The sexiest guy finalists. The promotion. Remember?"

"Vaguely."

"Well, they narrowed the list to four guys. A rocker. A model. Some writer who's got a hot book coming out. And listen to this, man, that actor, Bart Fitt."

"The one who goes around with his bottom hanging out?"

"That's the one. Susie's taking them all with her to Paris."

Matthew felt as if a giant fist had just landed in his solar plexus.

"We must have a bad connection," he said, very calmly. "Because I thought I heard you say—"

"You did. The whole bunch is going to Paris with her. See, this hotel's the place *CHIC*'s picked as their sexiest getaway, and Susie figures the way to get the most mileage is for her to represent Everywoman. I mean, that's the way she gears her column."

"Everywoman, how?" Matthew asked, trying to keep his voice steady even if his blood pressure wasn't.

"She'll spend the weekend with these four sexy guys. Eat with them, sleep with them—"

"*Sleep* with them?"

His voice rang out. People seated at the bar turned in his direction. Matthew turned his back.

"Well, not *sleep* with them. Take it easy, okay? I was speaking metaphorically."

"Yeah." Matthew took a breath, ran his hand through his hair. "Sorry, Joe. I, ah, I... So, how'd she react when you told her it was a no go?"

"A no-go?"

"I can just picture her face when you told her there wasn't a way in hell I'd let her spend a weekend in Paris with... Not a way in the world we'd approve such an expenditure."

The cell phone hummed with silence. Matthew's blood began humming, too.

"You did tell her that, didn't you?"

"Actually, I told her it sounded like a fantastic idea—"

"What?"

"—and that she had my blessings."

Matthew opened his mouth, then shut it. He strode through the cocktail lounge, weaving his way between tables, until he was standing beside Phoebe.

"Matthew?" she said. "Are you okay?"

Joe was saying the same words in his ear.

"I'm fine," Matthew replied, and drew back Phoebe's chair. "Joe?"

"Uh-huh?"

"Phone Hank. Tell him I'll be at the airport at midnight."

"Hank and the jet are in Tulsa. Remember? You told him to fly Frank down to check out that factory."

Matthew cursed under his breath. "Forget Hank. Call TWA. United. Air France. I don't care who, just get me to Paris."

"Paris?" Joe said.

"Paris?" Phoebe said.

Matthew forced a smile to his lips. "I'm afraid I've had a change of plans," he told a bewildered Phoebe as he signed the check, took her elbow and hustled her to the door. "Would you mind very much if I put you in a taxi and you saw yourself home?"

"Matt," Joe said, "are you nuts? You can't put me in a—"

"Not you," he growled, as he all but shoved Phoebe into a cab and stuffed bills into the driver's hand. The cab sped off, and Matthew glowered into the phone. "That was my date, you idiot. I put *her* into a cab, but *you* I'm going to put into an asylum. How could you tell Susannah it would be all right for her to take a—a male harem to Paris?"

"It's not a harem. It's a publicity stunt. I know it's a lot of money, but—"

"I don't give a flying fig about the money. My concern is strictly for—for the image of the magazine."

"You're joking, right?"

Matthew switched the phone to his other ear as the valet pulled his car to the curb.

"Did you ever consider what readers might think when they see a layout of *CHIC*'s editor, lying around in a Paris hotel room, being fawned over by a small army of—"

"Studly males?" Joe laughed. "I think they'll turn green with envy, Matt. And I think you're doing the same thing, although for very different reasons."

Matthew tipped the valet, got behind the wheel of his Porsche and shifted into gear.

"You really do belong in a straitjacket," he growled, and slapped the cell phone to silence.

CHAPTER NINE

MATTHEW stood in the customs line at Orly Airport and told himself to calm down.

He'd been telling himself the same thing for the past twenty minutes. Unfortunately, the message didn't seem to be getting through.

His plane was late, the line was long, there was an infant screaming somewhere up ahead...

It was fair to say he was not in a good mood.

Of all things for Joey to have done, he thought grimly. To have approved *CHIC*'s idiotically expensive, incredibly foolish scheme. What had his brother been thinking? *CHIC*, in Paris. Paris, of all places. From his brother's description, half the damn staff had flown over. A makeup guy. A hairdresser. A writer, a photographer, a stylist...

"Of course, first class," Joey had said, as if Matthew were crazy to ask. "What were we supposed to do? Fly Susannah and the four sexiest in first and the *CHIC* bunch in steerage?"

Susannah and the four sexiest. Matthew folded his arms and glowered. It sounded like a 1970s band, for heaven's sake. What a ridiculous promotion. What a dumb idea. What a senseless, silly, sorry, super-expensive excuse for boosting sales.

"Bah," Matthew muttered, as the line inched forward.

And he had nobody to blame but himself. He should have stayed with his gut instinct and shut *CHIC* down, or at the very least, he should have gone with what had made him as successful as he was. He was a man who knew how to delegate authority, but he also was known for keeping a close eye on new projects. That was what he should have done with *CHIC*, instead of handing its supervision to Joe, who probably knew as much about publishing as he knew about crocheting.

The bottom line was that Joey had let what should have

135

been a simple promotion gimmick get out of hand. And now he'd have to pay the price for his brother's carelessness.

The sexiest men alive. Matthew snorted. What nonsense! What drivel! Sexy restaurants, okay. Sexy hotels, sure. But sexy males? Living, breathing, sexy males?

"Stupid," he muttered, as the line shuffled forward.

Undeniably stupid. What had Joey been thinking of? Spending all that money. Sending Susannah to Paris with all those people.

Sending her there with four guys women all around the world probably dreamed of, when the only man Susannah ought to be dreaming of was—

"Monsieur?"

Matthew blinked. The French customs inspector was motioning him forward.

"Yes," Matthew said briskly, and stepped to the counter.

The sooner he cleared customs, the sooner he could be in the city. Then it was simply a matter of going to Le Grand Palais, setting the overreaching Miss Madison back on her heels and firmly pointing her and her hangers-on in the direction of home.

If those guys were really sexy, they could damned well be sexy over the conference table at the *CHIC* offices in New York. And he'd be there, too, to keep an eye on things.

The customs agent flipped open Matthew's passport.

"Welcome to France, monsieur. How long will you be with us?"

"No more than a day. Two, at the most."

"And is your trip a matter of business or pleasure, monsieur?"

Matthew's mouth thinned. "Business."

What other reason could he possibly have?

"Enjoy your stay, monsieur."

Matthew pocketed his passport. "I'm sure I will," he said grimly.

And he would. In fact, the thought of clipping Susannah's wings was enough to put a smile on his face for the first time in hours.

*   *   *

He made a brief stop at his hotel, a small, wonderfully old, quietly elegant place where the concierge knew him by name. A shower, a shave, a change of clothes, and he was on his way.

It was a perfect day—warm and sunny, with a soft breeze stirring the waters of the Seine. He decided to walk to Le Grand Palais. Paris was one of his favorite cities. Strolling the Champs Elysées and then l'Avenue Montaigne invariably soothed and refreshed his soul.

Not today.

The sights that usually made him smile—couples strolling arm in arm, lovers exchanging kisses—irritated the hell out of him. Couldn't people curb their displays? Why be so damned public about these things? *Behave yourself*, he wanted to snarl at the boy and girl locked in passionate embrace on a park bench.

Sanity returned with a rush. There was no reason to take his bad mood out on strangers—a bad mood due entirely to Joe's incompetence and Susannah's extravagance. Well, he'd take the situation in hand. There was nothing like the boss showing up in person to teach an insolent employee a lesson.

He marched through the lobby of Le Grand Palais, oblivious to the magnificent nineteenth-century décor. He'd phoned Joey from the plane, and his brother had provided the details. Susannah's suite was on the eighth floor. The Sexiests had their suites there, too.

"That way, nobody has to wear out the carpet, going back and forth from one suite to the other," Joey had said cheerfully.

"How thoughtful," Matthew had said coldly.

All the way up in the elevator, he thought about the look he would see on Susannah's face when she opened the door and found him standing there, the way she'd gasp when she realized that he wasn't going to let her play at being a Parisian courtesan on his time and at his expense.

It was time to establish exactly who was boss.

He stepped from the elevator, walked to the door of Susannah's suite and knocked. Then he folded his arms, settled his expression into one of cool disdain, and waited.

* * *

Susannah heard the knock at the door and tried hard not to shout hallelujah.

Thank you, she said silently to fate in the form of room service.

"One minute," she called gaily, and then she looked at her four companions. "Gentlemen? There's someone at the door."

Nobody heard her. Well, why would they? The underwear model, the rocker, the writer and the actor were all talking at once. They'd been doing that for the past two hours, and Susannah's head was spinning—especially since the travel agent who'd booked *CHIC* into Le Grand Palais had omitted one word from his description of the suite.

Magnificent, he'd said. Exquisite. Rococo.

It was all that. Unfortunately, it was also...

"Cozy," Claire had called it.

But the stylist deserved points for accuracy. "Whoa," she'd said, "this place gives me claustrophobia."

She was right.

Susannah was sharing a ten-by-twelve-foot sitting room with four impressively sized men, all of them handsome and all of them determined to stake a claim on her interest. She'd invited them for coffee so they could get to know each other and establish some sort of rapport.

It hadn't worked. The Sexiests weren't interested in rapport, they were interested in self-promotion, and that made them interested in her. She could almost read their minds.

If I can convince this woman that I'm the sexiest guy alive, each man was thinking, *my asking price will go sky-high.*

She'd been trying to look attentive and she supposed it was working, because the Sexiests were still babbling away, but she couldn't help wondering what they'd say if they knew all she was thinking about was how she'd managed to get herself into this mess.

Four men, one weekend, one cramped but elegant sitting room.

If this was what it was like to be the center of so much masculine attention, she could definitely do without it.

Alejandro, the underwear model, told her she had beautiful eyes.

Bart, the actor, said she was his soul mate.

Zeke, the rocker, promised that she would be the inspiration for his next song.

Stefan, the writer, assured her that he was going to dedicate his next novel to her.

And through it all, Susannah kept smiling, smiling and reminding herself that a weekend was only two days long even if the past half hour had felt like half a century.

If only the room were larger. If only she'd suggested meeting in the hotel's lounge. If only the sofa weren't built for midgets.

She sat in its elegant center, tucked between Alejandro with his hot, dark, dangerous smile, and Bart, with his inch-long lashes. At her feet sat Zeke, gazing at her soulfully and humming snatches of his newest hit. Stefan lounged against the wall, occasionally stroking his black, shoulder-length curls and throwing her sizzling glances.

The knock at the door had come just in time. All she had to do was manage to extricate herself from between Alejandro and Bart.

"The door," she said again, and struggled to her feet.

The Sexiests stood up, too, and purred her name in chorus.

It was at just that moment that Matthew, standing in the corridor, lost patience. How many times did a man have to knock before he was granted admittance? His eyes narrowed. Especially when he was the one paying for the hotel room.

He put his hand on the knob. It turned, the door swung open, and he saw Susannah for the first time in more than two weeks.

His first thought was that something was wrong with his heart. Why should it suddenly be going up and down in his chest? That was not what hearts were supposed to do, and it couldn't have a damn thing to do with the fact that no, Susannah wasn't as beautiful as he'd remembered...

She was more beautiful.

His second thought was that there was something wrong with not just his heart but his vision. How else to explain the fact that the room of this pay-off-the-national-debt-in-a-month suite was so damned tiny? On second glance, it wasn't his vision. The room was small, all right, but what made it seem even smaller was all the muscle that filled it.

Susannah was standing in front of a Lilliputian-size couch, flanked by a pair of giants, one dark, one fair. Another guy stood maybe a couple of feet way. He had curls—curls?—hanging to his shoulders. And there was a dude out in front who looked like an ad for steroids.

"Matthew?" Susannah breathed, and just for a heartbeat, for one infinitesimal second, he thought he saw her eyes fill with joy.

But he was wrong. It wasn't joy, it was shock. Of course, he thought coldly. She would be shocked. She had no reason to think he'd come along to shut down her weekend in paradise.

"Matthew," she said, "what on earth are you doing here?"

She stepped forward, her boy toys in lockstep with her.

"Yeah," the one with the curls said. "Susie Q? Didn't you say there were just four of us?"

"Yes. Yes, I did. This man isn't—he's not—"

"You heard the lady," Zeke said. "So, what are you doin' here, man?"

"I'm sorry," Matthew said pleasantly, "I'm afraid I don't know your name."

"Zeke. Zeke McCool."

Matthew smiled. "Is that supposed to mean something to me?" he said even more pleasantly. He could see that Curly was not happy. For that matter, neither were the two giants or the guy on steroids. They all looked as if they wanted a piece of him.

His smile curled into something that would have done a tiger proud. Considering his mood, what this foursome wanted sounded just fine.

"Matthew," Susannah said, her voice rising, "I asked you a question. What are you doing here?"

Matthew smiled at her. She blanched. Amazing how rewarding it was to know that a smile could cause that.

"I'm here to check on my investment, Madison. Why else?"

"What's he talking about?" Giant One asked suspiciously. "Susannah, you said there would only be four of us."

"There are. Four of us. Four of you." Susannah licked her lips. Matthew's appearance, so unexpected, so unwanted, so—

so magnificent, seemed to have obliterated her ability to think straight.

"Is this man your friend?"

"No. No, he's not my friend—"

"I'm her employer," Matthew said, looking around the room, smiling his toothy smile at each boy toy in turn. He could practically picture the adrenaline pumping through his veins. "The man who pays the bills. Anything else you guys want to know?"

Alejandro stepped forward. So did the others. Oh, yeah, Matthew thought. He grinned, bounced once on his toes and moved farther into the room.

Holy hell, thought Susannah, and leaped between the Sexiests and her boss.

"Now, stop this," she demanded. "Matthew, what's going on here?"

"I'll tell you what's going on," he said, his eyes never leaving the faces of the boy toys. "I'll tell you exactly what's going on, Madison. I found out about your little party—"

"My what?"

"Oh, give me a break! Save that innocent look for my brother, okay? Your fun and games weekend. Your bacchanalia. Your sexy guys party."

"Bacchanalia?" she asked. "Party?"

"You heard me. And after I chewed Joe out for being jerk enough to let you talk him into this—"

"Into what?"

"This," Matthew said, waving his hand so that it took in the room and the glowering quartet of muscle. "That's why I'm here, Madison. I flew here to—"

To what?

The torrent of words dried to a trickle, then stopped. Matthew felt a sick feeling welling in his throat. The four muscled hunks were looking at him as if he'd escaped from someplace that specialized in padded walls. Susannah was staring at him as if padded walls wouldn't be enough. And he was starting to think they were right.

Why did I come here? he thought furiously. *Why?*

"I came here," he said, "to, ah, to…"

Damnation. For the first time in his life, Matthew found

himself wishing the ground would open under his feet and swallow him whole. Susannah and the Sexiests were waiting for his answer, and he didn't have any. Why had he come here? It was not just a good question, it was the only question.

Susannah had told him she was going to run three issues of *CHIC*. Three special issues. She'd spice them up. Sex them up. Catch the attention of the advertisers and the readers. And he'd said go for it. He'd said he'd back her all the way. Then he'd handed the job to Joe and told his brother to give *CHIC*, and Susannah, whatever they needed.

Susannah's first issue had hit the stands, and it was a success. Now she had two more to go, and they'd sell even better. Susannah knew it. Joey knew it. Dammit, even he knew it.

Matthew frowned.

What *was* he doing here, then? He'd told Joe it was because of the cost of the Paris weekend, but who was he kidding? The money was a drop in the bucket, compared to what Romano Inc. spent in a day. Besides, it took money to make money.

The writer, the photographer, the whole bunch of people had nothing to do with his anger. Susannah could have had Eddie from the mail room tag along and he wouldn't have blinked. He hadn't come because of the people she'd brought here or because of the trip's price tag.

Matthew puffed out his breath.

He'd come because of Susannah. Because, dammit, if any man was going to take her to the world's most romantic city, it wasn't going to be this—this assemblage of over-hormoned hunks, this gaggle of Greek gods...

This sad little knot of confused guys who'd been flown here to be interviewed and photographed and, instead, were watching a man make a complete ass of himself in front of a woman he'd run from.

"Matthew?" Susannah said again, and he sighed, pasted what he hoped was a smile on his lips and said the only thing he could think of, that he'd flown to Paris because Joey had urged him to.

"Your brother asked you to come?"

"Yes. Ah..." *Ah, what?* "Ah, Joey said—he said that he trusted your judgment completely but that—that for something this big, he really thought it would be best to have your publisher on hand, just in case.''

He held his breath, waiting for her to ask, in case of what? But she didn't. Maybe she was still too angry to think logically. And she was angry. He could see it. Her face was flushed, her eyes were bright, her hands were planted on her hips. She looked angry and annoyed...

And lovely. So lovely. Why had he walked away from her that night? Why hadn't he realized there was only one way for the fire between them to burn itself out?

"You said..." Susannah cocked her head, as if to pin him with a glance. "You said this was a party. A—''

"A bacchanalia, whatever that is," the guy with the steroid problem said helpfully.

"Uh, yeah." Matthew nodded and told himself he'd only lose ground if he gave in to temptation, grabbed Steroid by the collar and tossed him into the hall. "Yeah, I did. But I was just quoting Joe."

Susannah stared at him. "Your brother told you this was a party?''

"No," he said quickly, "no, of course not. He said—he said this *wasn't* going to be a party. He said you'd insisted you didn't need any help with this project." Was it true? And, if it wasn't, could he confuse the issue enough to make it sound true? "He said you were just kidding yourself if you really thought you could do the interviews, the photos, the whole bit in just two days. So I figured I'd fly over to, ah, to offer my help."

"Your help," Susannah said.

"Exactly. I can pitch in. Assist. Offer my expertise."

"On what?''

Matthew frowned. The woman was a font of excellent, if unanswerable, questions.

"All right, Susannah. I'll tell it to you straight."

"I wish you would."

"I'm, uh, I'm trying not to hurt your feelings but the thing is, you've taken on a hell of a responsibility here." Yes. Yes, he was on the right track now. Matthew opened his jacket, thrust his hands into the pockets of his trousers and strolled into the room. He could hear the hunks shifting their weight behind him, turning so they could watch his every move. "A hell of a responsibility," he said, and swung to face the little group. *Joe,* he thought, *forgive me.* "And Joe and I have some concerns."

Susannah dug her hands into her pockets, too.

"Concerns?"

"Yes. This project is really important to the magazine. You're on a tight deadline. And you're new to this. I'm sure you can understand that Joe and I discussed this and decided we'd feel better if one of us were on-site with you in Paris."

Susannah cocked her head again. He knew she was trying to decide whether or not to believe him, but what could she do even if she didn't? She was here. He was here. That, therefore, was that.

"Then why did you come? Why not your brother?"

"Joe's in Miami. On business." That much was true. It wouldn't serve any point to add that Joe's business involved a much-deserved two weeks of sun and fun with his latest redhead. "I, on the other hand, was able to free up the next few days." Matthew smiled ingratiatingly. "So here I am."

Susannah nodded. So here he was, she thought. Here he was, and she still wasn't sure if she'd wanted to throw herself into his arms that first minute or if she'd wanted to have one of the Sexiests shove him into the corridor so she could slam the door in his face and pretend she'd never seen him.

Her throat constricted.

Who was she trying to kid? The only thing she was certain of was that her heart had gone into overdrive when Matthew stepped into the room. She'd missed him. Oh, how she'd missed him...

"Susannah?"

She looked around. Zeke had come sidling up behind her. He was looking at Matthew as if Matthew were some strange species no one had ever seen before.

"Yes?"

"Is this guy who he says he is?" Zeke asked out of the side of his mouth. "'Cause, if he isn't, you just say the word and—"

"He is," Susannah said quickly. She smiled and put her hand on Zeke's arm. "He's definitely who he says he is. Let me introduce you. Everybody? This is my boss, Matthew Romano. Mr. Romano—Matthew, this is Zeke McCool, Stefan Zyblos, Bart Fitt and Alejandro Rio.''

The Sexiests stepped up, one by one, and gripped Matthew's hand. He wondered if it were deliberate, the hard press of fingers and flesh, decided it was, and gave back as good as he got.

"Delighted," he said, and smiled.

"You came close, Romano," Alejandro Rio said.

"Close?"

Rio flashed Susannah a hot, dark and dangerous smile. "We weren't going to let you push our lady around, were we, *compadres?*"

Matthew smiled, too. "I'm sure you weren't." He stepped forward and slipped an arm around Susannah's shoulders. He felt her stiffen, but she stood her ground. "And I'm happy to know that *my* lady was so well-cared for in my absence."

Susannah swung toward him. "Your lady?" she spluttered.

The warning was clear. Matthew heard it in her voice, saw it in the sudden blaze of anger in her eyes, felt it in the way she tried, suddenly, to pull free of his arm. But he'd gone too far to stop now, and besides, he didn't want to stop. Not with all the testosterone floating in the air.

"Susie, sweetheart," he said softly, "I know we've always agreed on the importance of discretion, but these—gentlemen—are entitled to the truth, don't you think? Besides, this is Paris. The city of lovers. Why should we pretend, hmm?"

And, still smiling, he bent his head and kissed her.

CHAPTER TEN

SUSANNAH sat at a table at the sidewalk café just outside Le Grand Palais, sipping what remained of a cup of café Americaine.

Two tables away, Matthew was putting Bart and Alejandro, Zeke and Stefan through their paces. It was an amazing sight. Any minute now, she expected the four Sexiests to roll over, sit and stay on command, and why?

Susannah's eyes glittered with tightly suppressed anger.

Because Matthew Romano ordered it, that was why.

What ill wind had blown him back into her life? A few hours ago, Matthew had been the Unseen Publisher. Now he was in her space. In her hair. In her way. Just remembering the performance he'd put on in the suite made her want to shriek with fury.

"How dare you kiss me?" she'd hissed as soon as they'd had a moment alone, and he'd given her a look of schoolboy innocence and explained that he'd assessed the situation and immediately realized that instead of focusing their energies on the camera, the Sexiests would focus it on her unless they realized she was already spoken for.

"That's ridiculous," she'd snapped, and Matthew had patted her cheek indulgently, smiled and said she just didn't understand.

It was, he said, a male thing.

A male thing, indeed, she thought sourly. It was a macho thing, was what he'd meant. With that one kiss, he'd established himself as the man in charge. Suddenly, he was an expert on photography, on style, on what would attract readers and what wouldn't. And everybody believed him, from the Sexiests to the makeup guy. Even Claire had joined the enemy camp, judging by the way she sighed as she slipped into the chair alongside Susannah's.

"He's so creative, Suze," she whispered. "Isn't it amazing?"

Susannah gave her a disgusted look. "Amazing."

"And so handsome!"

"Is he? I hadn't noticed."

"And so sexy!"

Enough was enough. Susannah glared at Claire.

"How can you let him take you in?" she demanded. "The man's a conceited, arrogant, insufferable egomaniac. And he's about as sexy as an—an eggplant, compared to Alejandro and Bart and Zeke and—"

"Susannah?"

Susannah looked up. The arrogant, insufferable egomaniac himself was standing over her. If he'd overheard what she'd just said, he wasn't letting it show. He looked as deep in creative thought as a Broadway director on a busy day.

"Are you talking to me?" she asked politely.

"Jimmy's pointed out that we haven't had you in any of the photographs."

Susannah smiled with all her teeth. "Is that right?"

"I know you'd planned things differently."

"Well, yes. Yes, we had. We'd spent days and days organizing what you've managed to tear apart in an afternoon...but don't let that bother you, Mr. Romano. You are, after all, God."

"Suze," Claire whispered, and put her hand on Susannah's arm, but Susannah shook off both the hand and the warning.

"So don't worry about me not being in any of the photos. Don't concern yourself with the hours of time that went into setting up this weekend. And, most especially, don't bother yourself with how our readers will want to see me as their link to the four Sexiests. Please empty your mind of all concerns." She smiled again, even more brilliantly. "You do have a mind, don't you, Mr. Romano?"

It was, she was pleased to see, a direct hit. Claire made a sound like someone trying to swallow a whale, and Matthew...oh, yes. Matthew's carefully assumed look of creative angst collapsed like an ice sculpture under the unwelcome attentions of a blowtorch, revealing the man beneath—a man whose eyes snapped with anger.

"She didn't mean that," Claire said quickly.

"She did." Matthew's voice was a study in control. "But I can understand her pique."

"You can?"

"Of course. Miss Madison planned this—this exercise with the greatest care."

"Oh, she did," Claire babbled, "she definitely did."

Matthew's jaw tightened. "A weekend in Paris with four—what was the word Miss Madison used to describe our finalists?"

"Sexiests," Claire supplied. "We call them the four—"

"Sexiests. A charming description, especially for Miss Madison, who would have had a hotel suite, complete with her very own stag line, all expenses paid by me."

"Paid out of my budget," Susannah said hotly, "all of it necessary for *CHIC* and, just to remind you, Miss Madison does not appreciate being discussed in the third person."

"Necessary?" Matthew asked with a smirk.

"Necessary," Susannah said, kicking back her chair and standing to confront him. "We've been promoting this weekend and the sexiest man alive for some time. How you can manage to make this sound like—like some half-baked scheme I've come up with for my own amusement is beyond me!"

It was beyond him, too. Matthew stared into the enraged, beautiful face of his editor-in-chief. She was right on all counts, and he knew it. This wasn't a weekend of fun and games, it was work. Hard work. He'd reminded himself of that as the *CHIC* crew had trooped from one shooting location to another, reminded himself of it as he'd watched Susannah have her hair fixed and her nose powdered...

Reminded himself of it as he'd watched the photographer pose her with the four hunks of muscle.

Oh, yeah, he surely had watched that, long enough so the images were probably forever burned into his brain.

Susannah on the steps of L'Opera, smiling for the camera as the four Sexiests gathered around her like piranhas in a feeding frenzy.

Susannah at a metro stop, laughing as Alejandro lifted her in his arms and whirled her in a circle .

Susannah in the lobby of Le Grand Palais, caught between

Zeke and Bart as they each pressed a kiss to her blushing cheeks.

"Oh, you're all such sweethearts," she'd said, at which point Matthew had made a decision.

He could watch Susannah laugh and smile and have a good time with the four overgrown, overmuscled, oversexed pretty boys and end up in a straitjacket, or he could rationally, reasonably and intelligently point out that the layout, as they'd planned it, just wasn't going to work.

And so he'd called them all together, sat them down in Susannah's suite—the corporate suite, as he now referred to it—and he'd explained, with the same touch of concern in his voice he used when he explained things to the worried executives of failing corporations, that *CHIC* had made a mistake.

"I know," he'd said gently, "that you think this is going to work. Letting your readers experience this weekend through Susannah, I mean."

"Well, sure," Claire had said, and Matthew had sighed, looked to the ceiling, and shaken his head with regret.

"I'm afraid not."

Susannah hadn't spoken. She'd sat across from him, her face giving nothing away. Claire, however, had leaped to her feet.

"Of course it'll work. Maybe Suze hasn't explained it completely. She's...how can I put it? She's our readers' surrogate, Matthew. She's their conduit to pleasure."

The picture that artful phrase had put into his head had been enough to make him want to abduct Susannah and hide her away forever. Instead, he'd spouted some nonsense about how readers would feel if Susannah, their dear friend and guide to sexy pleasures, turned out to be the focus of the finalists' attentions.

"They'll feel cheated," he'd said solemnly. "As if someone had stolen their fantasy."

There'd been a silence. Claire had looked at Susannah, Susannah had looked at Claire, they'd both looked at the photographer...

"He's right," the photographer had said. "It's like that ad campaign for Lollapalooza Lipsticks, you know? Where they shot the movie star and his latest love? The company figured every woman in the world would buy their stuff, but it didn't work out. Chicks took one look at the guy's lady and thought, well, if she's got him, what hope is there for me?''

"But this isn't like that," Susannah said, and then, all at once, everybody was talking, even the hairdresser, all of them looking at Matthew as if he'd just discovered the cure for the common cold, and what could she say that wouldn't have sounded as if she were upset about being shut out of the photos? And, dammit, it had nothing to do with that. If anything, Matthew's pronouncement had come as a relief.

She hadn't stopped to think what it would be like, having the camera focus on her, having Jimmy telling her to smile, to flirt, to tilt her head. The Sexiests were turning out to be nice guys, nicer than she'd expected, but they were accustomed to the flash of the camera. She wasn't.

In fact, she'd found that she hated it.

And yet, she didn't hate the camera half as much as she hated Matthew. Oh, he'd given her an explanation for his being here, but she didn't buy it. What was the real reason? He'd trusted her with *CHIC* until now, so what had changed? Was he really so convinced she'd mess up that he'd felt it necessary to come marching onto her turf? Or was he simply determined to do what he'd sworn not to do—to undermine her authority?

She wasn't about to ask him. And she wasn't going to knuckle under. She would be a constant, silent, critical presence.

At least, that had been her intention.

Now, glowering at him over the circumference of a tiny, glass-topped table, her resolve was slipping.

"You're making a mistake," she said icily. "You can bark out all the orders you want, but you're doing this all wrong."

Everyone fell silent and stared at her.

"Now, wait just a minute, Madison…"

"No. No, *you* wait, Romano." And then, because business was business and anger was anger and the two had nothing to do with each other, she tossed him a bone. "All right. Maybe you were right about readers not wanting to see me with the Sexiests."

Matthew's brows lifted. "Maybe?"

"But they'll want to see something. Someone. Some girl dancing with Zeke or looking into Bart's eyes."

Matthew frowned. "You know, you just might be right."

For a moment, she thought he might be about to apologize. Instead, he turned toward Claire.

"Do we have contacts at any French modeling agencies?"

"French modeling..." Claire frowned. "Yes. Yes, we do. I've dealt with this one place."

"Call them. Ask them to send over..." Matthew looked at the four Sexiests, who were trying to look inconspicuous. "Fellas? Blonde? Brunette? Redhead? If you have preferences, sing out now."

"One of each," Zeke said, with a grin.

Everybody but Susannah laughed.

"You heard the man," Matthew said. "Only make it two of each, so we can be sure we get only the best."

Night was falling over Paris.

Susannah stood at the window in her sitting room. She'd showered, washed her hair, put on a long, pink silk robe, and now she was toasting the sun as it set behind the chimney-pot rooftops.

"Cheers," she said softly, and lifted her glass of diet cola to the sight.

It had been one hell of a long, terrible day, but now it was over. Tomorrow morning, her finalists and the French models would head for Versailles and the first of six photo shoots. She'd never been there, but she'd seen pictures of the palace. It was magnificent. The Sexiests would do it proud...and so would the girls Matthew had hired.

He had certainly put himself into his work.

Susannah frowned and took another sip.

"You do the interviewing, Madison," he'd said, with a pompous, aren't-I-generous smile.

"Don't be silly, Mr. Romano," she'd said, with a smile that more than matched his. "You do it. You're the expert on blondes, but I'm sure you can handle redheads and brunettes if you put your mind to it. I'll just sit here and take notes."

The bastard hadn't had the good sense to know she was

insulting him. He'd simply shrugged, said they'd do it whatever way she liked and told Claire to send in the first girl.

The first was a DB. No surprise there.

"And what is your name, mademoiselle?" Matthew had asked, purring.

"Yvette, monsieur." Yvette had giggled. "And I understand it would please you to have me be of some service."

Service, indeed, Susannah had thought.

Matthew had given her a sexy grin. "Just hold that thought, Yvette," he'd said.

There was more give-and-take, but Susannah had tuned out. Why listen to a man make an ass of himself over a woman? Why pay attention to a woman making a fool of herself over a man?

Yvonne followed Yvette, Clara followed Claudette, blah, blah, blah. Susannah had participated by yawning. Matthew was in charge. Let him pick the winners.

Or let the winners pick him.

"I am late for an appointment, monsieur," a blonde with big violet eyes had whispered in a bad imitation of Marilyn Monroe. "Perhaps we could conduct the rest of this interview this evening…if monsieur should be interested, that is."

And she'd bent low over the desk, low enough so her breasts had threatened to bounce out of her dress, and handed Matthew a card with her address scrawled across it.

Susannah paced away from the window.

That was probably where he was now. Celebrating in his own fashion. Everyone else had gone out to dinner. Claire had phoned to ask her to join them.

"You don't have to worry about clashing with Matthew, either," she'd added. "He begged off."

Of course, he'd begged off. Why would he choose to spend an evening battling with her when he could be out dancing with Claudette or Yvonne? Or not dancing. Maybe they were sipping champagne. Maybe they were dining by candlelight. Maybe they were—maybe they were…

"Stop it," Susannah whispered angrily.

What did it matter? Matthew could do what he liked, where he liked, with whom he liked. She certainly didn't care. He was her employer, and business didn't mix with pleasure.

Tears blurred her vision. She shook her head, wiped her hand across her eyes. What was there to cry about? She'd made wonderful progress in her career. Her life was going exactly the way she wanted it.

There was a knock at the door. Susannah sighed. It had to be Claire. She meant well, but she just wouldn't take no for an answer.

"Just a minute," she yelled.

Quickly, she detoured into the bathroom, snatched a tissue from the vanity and dabbed at her eyes. She ran her hands through her hair, fixed what she hoped would be a passable smile to her lips and hurried to the door.

"Claire," she said, as she opened it, "really, I don't feel—"

But it wasn't Claire. It was Matthew. Matthew, looking heart-stoppingly handsome in a dark suit and with a bouquet of flowers in his hand.

Flowers? For her? Her heart did one of the silly flips it had done weeks ago, the night he'd taken her to dinner at the Gilded Carousel.

"Susannah," he said politely.

"Matthew," she said, every bit as politely.

He cocked his head. "Are you okay?"

"Yes," she said, with a little laugh, "I'm fine."

"You look as if you've been crying."

"Crying? Me? No, don't be silly. I—I just got out of the shower, that's all. There's shampoo in my eyes."

"Oh." He glanced at his watch. "May I come in? I'll only be a minute. I have—an appointment."

The wispy flutter of hope, which was what it had been, even though it was agony to admit it, died a quick death in her breast.

"I understand," she said brightly.

"And you? Are you going out this evening with one of our heroes?" His tone was flat and made the word sound foolish, but she smiled as if she hadn't noticed.

"You frightened them off, remember?"

"And a good thing, too. We have an early start tomorrow."

Susannah's false smile faded. Why had her heart been doing

flips? It was her stomach that should have flipped at the presence of Matthew the Insolent.

"Actually, Alejandro asked me if you and I were really seeing each other. I explained that that kiss was your idea of a little joke, and he said he might drop by for a drink later this evening."

"Alejandro," he said. His lip curled. "Doesn't Sam mind?"

"Excuse me?"

"Sam." Matthew's eyes were dark. "You do remember Sam, don't you? How would he feel if he knew you were going to spend the evening with another man?"

Susannah flushed. "I know it's difficult for you to comprehend, but spending the evening with Alejandro doesn't mean spending the night. Besides, Sam and I have an...understanding."

"And Peter? Do you and he have an understanding, too?"

"Is that why you came here? To interrogate me about Sam and Peter?"

"I'm just curious, Madison. Your lovers seem to have a very liberated attitude toward fidelity and commitment."

She laughed. "You're a fine one to talk about fidelity and commitment."

"We're not talking about me," he said. And, even if they had been, she was wrong. One at a time, was his motto. For a week. A month. Two months, if the woman was really special. Nonna, during one of her lectures on the importance of finding a wife, had once accused him of being afraid to make a commitment to a woman, but it wasn't true. He just—he wasn't ready to give up the joys of bachelorhood, that was all.

"At least I don't keep two women dangling on the same string," he said coldly.

"I'm sure you're a candidate for sainthood, Mr. Romano. Fortunately, it's a free country, and I don't have to answer to anybody. Now, if you'll excuse me?"

She started to shut the door, but Matthew jammed his foot in the way.

"Maybe that's your problem. Maybe you need a man who wouldn't accept that kind of answer."

"I'm not interested in that kind of relationship."

"Why not?" He smiled, and the smile sent a sudden warning heat racing through her blood. "Afraid somebody like that would be too much for you to handle?" He reached out, ran a finger lightly from her temple to her throat. "I'll bet nobody's ever tapped into that fire trapped inside you."

She knew better than to tell him there was no fire. He'd kissed her, he'd felt her ignite in his arms. There was nothing she could do to wipe away the knowledge, but he must never know that the fire had shocked her as much as it had shocked him, that all it would take to set it blazing again was the stroke of his hand on her skin.

They looked at each other, and the world stopped. Everything had changed. There was no teasing glint in his eyes, no taunting smile on his lips. All she had to do was move, tilt her face for his kiss...

Susannah jerked back, terrified. Her pulse was racing. She wondered if he could see its telltale thump in the hollow of her throat.

"Did you come here for a reason, Romano? A business reason? If you did, let's hear it. If not, get out."

Her voice trembled. Matthew wanted to think it was with desire, but he knew better. It trembled with anger, and the realization shattered the sexual haze that had engulfed him.

Dammit, he thought furiously, what was going on here? He'd come to apologize for usurping her authority. For giving her a bad day. For making an ass of himself by turning everything upside down, and all because he couldn't watch her laugh and play and have a good time with those four harmless, silly, muscle-bound boys. Not that he was going to tell her that. What was the point? Susannah and he were like oil and water. Forget the sizzle. There was no way they'd ever really connect.

"I'm waiting, Romano. And time is running out."

He looked at her. She was barefoot. Without shoes on, she didn't even come up to his chin. Her face was scrubbed, her hair was damp, she was clutching the lapels of her robe as if he were an Aztec high priest and she were a virginal sacrifice.

Something knotted deep in his belly. *Get out,* every instinct in him screamed, *get out, Romano, get out!*

He took a step back. "Here," he said gruffly, and shoved

the bouquet at her. She looked at it as if she thought it might be hiding a beehive.

"What's that?"

"Dammit, Madison, what do you think it is?"

"Flowers?" she said. Puzzlement shone in her eyes. "For me?"

Matthew blew out his breath. "I'm standing at your door with a bouquet in my hand. Who else would it be for?"

"Well, I thought—I assumed the flowers were for—for whichever of those girls you're seeing tonight."

"Girls? Oh. Oh, the models." He ran his hand through his hair. "I'm not seeing…I'm not picking up, ah, Bernadette, until later."

"Bernadette? Was there a Bernadette at the interviews this afternoon?"

Was there? Damned if he knew. The interviews had been a nightmare. All those overly made-up females, with their cleavage and their hair…

"Yes. No. I mean… Look, it's a peace offering, okay? There's no sense in you and me going at each other the rest of the time we're here. We both want what's best for *CHIC*, right?"

Susannah nodded. "Of course."

"Then take the flowers. We'll shake hands, I'll leave, and you can wait for Bart to drop by."

"Zeke."

Matthew frowned. "Bart. Or Alejandro. I'm sure you never mentioned Zeke."

"Alejandro said Zeke might stop by, too," she said quickly. "Anyway, it doesn't matter." She looked up and smiled. "I'll take them."

"What?"

"The flowers. You're right, it's foolish for us to argue. Thank you," she said formally, as she accepted the bouquet. "It was nice of you to think of me."

Nice of him? Nice? Matthew swallowed hard. He thought of her all the time. Dreamed of her. Imagined what it would be like to take her in his arms.…

Which was nonsense. Even if he set aside his rules about business mixed with pleasure, why would he want to get involved with a woman like Susannah? She was prickly and obstinate. She'd surely put her career ahead of anything else, ahead of him. Not that that would matter. The last thing he needed was a woman who wanted more of him than he was willing to give.

"Have a scent."

He blinked. Susannah was smiling at him over the roses.

"Sorry? I, ah, I missed that."

"I said, the roses have a scent. They never do, at home."

Roses she got from Sam? From Peter? "I'm glad you like them." He held out his hand. "Friends?"

Susannah hesitated. "Not enemies, at least," she said, and smiled.

He smiled, too. His hand closed around hers. Her skin was cool, but when she tilted her head and looked at him, her eyes were smoky.

"Well," he said.

"Well," she said.

"Good night, Susannah."

"Good night, Matthew."

He turned. She put her hand on the doorknob. He stepped into the hall. She began to shut the door...

"The hell with this," he growled, and swung toward her. "Dammit, Susannah," he said, and before his heart could take another beat, she was in his arms.

He lifted her, and she wound her arms around his neck as his hand tunneled into her hair. He kicked the door shut and kissed her without preliminaries, without gentleness. Why would there be wooing when they both knew that this moment had been inevitable?

"Alejandro's not coming, is he?" he said, his mouth a breath from hers.

Susannah shook her head. "Bernadette?"

"There is no Bernadette."

She laughed, but the laugh became a moan as his mouth covered hers. His hands were everywhere, stroking her beneath the silk robe, fingers excitingly rough and hot .

"No more games, Susannah."

"No," she whispered, stroking the tip of her tongue against

his, reveling in the heavy beat of his heart against hers. "No more games, Matthew."

He tasted of danger and of darkness. Of the heady wildness of desire.

She tasted of hunger and of need. Of the sweetness of passion.

"I want—I want—"

"Everything," he whispered, and kissed her again.

"Yes. Oh, yes."

She dragged his jacket off his shoulders. He ripped away his tie. She slid her hands under his shirt, thrilling at the sharp intake of his breath, at the sound he made when she swept her palms over his muscled chest.

"Matthew," she said, her voice breaking, "Matthew..."

Her hands clenched in his hair as he lifted her again and carried her to the bedroom, to the canopied bed. Her heart thundered as he eased her down the length of his aroused body. Her toes curled into the deep carpet as he slid her robe from her shoulders. It fell around her in a waterfall of pink silk, exposing her to his gaze.

"Sweet Susannah," he whispered, and framed her face in his hands.

She looked at him, her eyes wide with wonder. Carefully, as if she were some fragile work of art, he bent to her, sucked her bottom lip between his teeth, bit gently as she sighed his name and sighed again as his mouth traveled the length of her throat. She was a creature of pounding blood and shimmering fire. Her head fell back. She needed his strength to support her, and he gave it, lifting her, holding her to him before laying her gently on the bed.

He rose above her. She watched from under her lashes as he removed his shirt, baring the hard muscles of his shoulders and chest. Her breath caught when he undid his belt and peeled off the rest of his clothing, revealing the shadowed planes that were the magnificence and power of his male body.

"Look at me, Susannah," he said, his voice husky with desire.

She did, forcing open eyes heavy with passion, fixing her gaze on his taut features as he cupped her breasts.

"My beautiful Susie," he whispered. "My lovely Susannah."

"Matthew," she sighed, "oh, Matthew..."

"Say my name again."

"Matthew. Matthew, Matthew, Matth—"

He crushed her mouth beneath his, then bent his dark head and gently rubbed his stubbled chin over the soft, sensitive flesh of her breasts. When his lips closed first around one pebbled nipple and then the other, she arced toward him.

"Do you like that?" he whispered. "Tell me, Susie. Tell me what pleases you."

"You," she said, lifting her arms to him, "you, always—"

He kissed her again and again. She could feel the heat in him, smell his excitement, feel the heat of her passion and how it had turned her wet and ready for him. But she had always been ready for him, from that first day, from some time that existed only in the dark, dim past.

Now, at last, the waiting was ended.

"Now," she pleaded. "Matthew, please, I want—I need—"

She rose to him, her arms clinging to his neck, her mouth hot, and he buried himself deep, deep within her on one long, hard, exquisite thrust. A sweet cry of surrender broke from her throat as he possessed her.

"Oh, yes," she sobbed, "Matthew, Matthew..."

"Susannah," he said, "my Susannah," and then he was moving, moving, and she was flying into the sun, splintering, shattering until, at last, she was whole.

Whole, and in Matthew's arms.

CHAPTER ELEVEN

MATTHEW awoke slowly from the most erotic dream he'd ever had.

The dream had been about Susannah, about a long, incredible night shared with her. He'd made love to her, with her, in all the ways a man and a woman could possibly make love.

Except, it wasn't a dream.

Susannah was right here, nestled in the curve of his arm. She lay on her side, her head on his shoulder. Her hand was curled in the middle of his chest. Her leg was draped across his. They must have been lying this way for quite some time, because his shoulder felt a bit stiff and his leg felt a little cramped.

It didn't matter. His muscles could end up screaming, for all he cared. What was a little muscle ache compared to the joy of having Susannah in his arms?

Carefully, he turned his head. He didn't want to wake her, he just wanted to look at her. To study that lovely profile with its dark sweep of lash. The sexy fullness of her lower lip. The elegant nose and feminine yet determined chin.

She was so beautiful. So very beautiful. How could he resist? He wouldn't really wake her, he'd just kiss her. Only one kiss. A gentle one.

He moved, shifting his weight so they were lying face to face. He stroked his hand over her hair, then all the way down her spine. Her skin was silken and warm, her bottom gently rounded. She stirred under his touch, sighed but didn't awaken.

"Sweet," he whispered, and brushed her mouth with his. "So sweet."

He had to be careful. He reminded himself that he really didn't want to wake her. She was sleeping so soundly, and it was enough for him just to lie here, to hold her. But her mouth was only a breath from his. And her breasts were so soft against his chest.

One more kiss. Just one. One more feathered caress.

He kissed her. Touched her. She came awake in his arms, her mouth eager under the questing pressure of his, and the need within him burned bright and fierce. He rolled her beneath him, and her sighs of pleasure became moans of passion.

"Matthew," she whispered, and she rose to meet his thrusts, rose to meet his kisses.

"Yes," he said, "yes," and as he held himself poised above her, prolonging that last, magical moment, he knew it was no use pretending this was only sex.

It was—it was...

Susannah sighed his name again, and moved against him. Matthew stopped thinking. He groaned her name, threw his head back, thrust even deeper and imploded in her arms.

Later, they sat at a small table near the window in the sitting room, Matthew wearing only his trousers, Susannah wearing the hotel's oversize terry-cloth robe.

The table was covered with starched white linen and spread with fine china and sterling flatware. A crystal vase filled with flowers stood amid serving dishes and baskets filled with fresh strawberries, cheeses, water biscuits and flaky *pain au chocolat.*

Susannah took a sip of her champagne. "This," she said, "is not Aunt Sally's."

Matthew chuckled. "Yeah, I'd say you were right."

"And this is not breakfast. Champagne. Chocolate. Strawberries."

"I agree. Breakfast is a glass of orange juice, a bowl of oatmeal, lots of bacon, four eggs, buttered toast..."

"Good grief! You have to be joking!"

Matthew grinned, sat back in his chair and reached for her hand.

"When your job means you wake up while it's still dark and cold, then head out into the Pacific on a trawler, you don't worry very much about calories or cholesterol."

"Whose job?" Susannah's eyes widened. "Yours?"

"Sure. It's what my old man did. It was what I figured to do, too, until I got lucky."

"Lucky how?"

He looked at her hand, lying curled within his.

"I'd like to tell you I was a brilliant student, that I was a Rhodes scholar and spent a year at Oxford." His eyes met hers, and he smiled. "But the truth is, I was big and tough, and I sacked enough quarterbacks on the teams my high school played to win myself a football scholarship to the University of Michigan. I figured I'd get lucky and end up playing for the pros. My old man thought it was a waste of my time and his income because he had to hire a kid to replace me." He shrugged. "So I made him a bet."

Susannah was sitting forward, her eyes fixed on his. "What kind of bet?"

"I said I'd ditch the scholarship, come home and work with him on his boat if I didn't tackle the quarterback as many times in the season as he came home with a full load of fish. Well, actually, it was a little more complicated than that. I worked out a formula that compared the probability of fish tonnage to getting to the quarterback. Anyway, I won, and Pop lost. He stopped giving my mother a hard time over my 'foolishness,' and I suddenly realized I could maybe do more with my head than use it to confuse an offensive lineman."

"And?"

Matthew looked at Susannah. Her eyes were bright. She was smiling as if she really gave a damn about the boy he'd been. He wasn't sure which surprised him more, that she'd be interested enough to listen or that he'd just told her stuff about himself nobody else knew.

Why had he done that? he thought, and the hair rose on the back of his neck just as it had that night, weeks ago, at the Gilded Carousel.

"And," he said lightly, "why am I sitting here, boring you to death with the story of my life when we should be finishing our champagne before it goes flat?"

Matthew didn't want to talk about himself anymore. Susannah understood that. She never talked about herself or her past, either...except for that night at the Gilded Carousel. A faint prickle of alarm raced along her skin. It was so easy to be with him. Not just to make love but to talk to him, listen to him, watch the animation in his face.

How simple it would be, she thought suddenly, to fall crazy in love with Matthew Romano.

"Susannah?" Matthew said, and when she met his gaze, she knew he'd seen something in her face. She worked hard to draw breath into her lungs, harder still to shove the terrifying thought aside and to smile.

"Yes?"

"You drifted away for a minute, Susie. Where'd you go?"

Where, indeed? She ran the tip of her tongue over her lips. "I—I was thinking that—that we have a meeting this morning."

A meeting? Matthew frowned. She was right, they did have a meeting scheduled. He had forgotten all about it, which was something he'd never done before. But Susannah had remembered. His smile faded. He should have known that she would not forget.

"A meeting. Of course."

"And soon. So—so I'll need to shower and dress."

His gaze swept over her, from her tousled curls down the robe to her bare feet.

"We both will." He rose and gently tugged her to stand beside him. "What kind of showerer are you, Madison? Hot? Cold? Warm?" He bent his head, brushed her lips with his. "These things are important, you know."

She knew what he was saying. He expected they'd shower together. But she couldn't. Not now. She'd slept with him, made passionate love with him, and it was too much. Her thoughts, her emotions were running away.

She needed time and space.

"I like my shower hot," she said, with a quick smile. "And, luckily for me, this hotel seems to have an unending supply of hot water." She took a deep breath. "How about your hotel? Will you get a hot shower this morning, or a tepid one?"

It was a direct hit. She saw the sudden narrowing of his eyes, knew he'd gotten the message—and that he didn't like it. *I don't like it, either,* she longed to cry out, *but I'm afraid, Matthew. I don't want to fall in love with you.*

"Am I being told, ever so courteously, that it's time I

packed my things and headed for my own quarters?'' he asked with a polite smile.

Susannah drew the lapels of her robe together.

''Well,'' she said, with an equally polite smile, ''well, you know how it is....''

''I don't think I do. Suppose you tell me.''

Damn him! He was making this difficult. Well, so be it. He was the one who'd pointed out that sex was sex and business was business.

''The meeting,'' she said.

Matthew stepped back and folded his arms over his bare chest. Muscles rippled in his shoulders, and she tried not to think about how hot his skin had felt under her palms.

''What about it?''

''It's going to be here. In this suite.''

''So?''

''So, if the suite's not made up, if that table is still set for two, if you're already here...''

''Yes?'' he said politely.

''They'll know.''

''Know what?''

''Matthew, for heaven's sake, must I spell it out?''

''Yes,'' he said coolly. ''You must.''

Susannah puffed out a breath. She crossed the room, then swung to face him, her arms outstretched.

''They'll know that we—that you and I... Dammit, Matthew! They'll know that we—that we...''

That we made love, he waited for her to say. And then he'd go to her, swing her into his arms, carry her to the bedroom and tell her he didn't care who in hell knew, that he was going to make love to her again, just to make sure her eyes glowed and her skin had the flushed look of a woman well-loved when the A-to-Z Sexiests came walking in.

''They'll know that we slept together,'' she said, in a strangled voice.

She said it the same way someone else might say, *They'll know that we stole the silverware.* A muscle knotted in his jaw. It should have been funny. He knew that. But the last thing he wanted to do was laugh.

She was right. They had slept together. It was a phrase he'd used often, a phrase he'd always felt comfortable with, even if what people did in bed together had little to do with sleep. But the other phrase, the one about making love, had always struck him as cloying and untrue. So why did it bother him, to hear "we slept together" coming from Susannah's soft, sweet mouth?

"Matthew? Did you hear me?"

"I heard you." He tried a smile. "It's not against the law, Susie, especially not here, in Paris."

"You know what I mean, Matthew. They'll know. And—"

"And your authority will be undermined."

His tone was flat and cold, as was the look in his eyes. No, she thought, oh, no. That wasn't what she meant, not at all. What they'd done had been so special. So wonderful. She wanted him to tell her that, to say, Susannah, we didn't sleep together, we made love. We made love, and it meant everything to me....

"Susannah? Is that the problem?"

Her head came up. She looked at him. "Yes," she said, because the lie was far, far safer than the truth. "It isn't that I'm—that I regret it."

Her words were rushed, tumbling from her lips like stones, but she couldn't stop them, even though she knew she was ruining everything, destroying the few days or weeks they might have shared—not that Matthew gave her the chance.

"There's no need to explain." He turned from her. She followed him into the bedroom, watched as he collected his scattered clothing. "I understand completely."

"Good," she said, in a tight voice. "I wouldn't want you to think—"

He looked at her, his face expressionless. "Think what? That business is business and sex is sex?"

"I didn't say that."

"You didn't have to. I did." He flashed a quick smile. "Phone housekeeping. Ask them to come up and do a quick cleaning. I'll be back in an hour. And, Susannah?"

"Yes?" she said, and tried for the same even tone as his.

He smiled again. "Thank you for reminding me just how things are."

He buttoned his shirt, slipped on his jacket, tucked his tie into his pocket and walked out, closing the bedroom door after him.

Susannah stared at the closed door.

Well, that had been easy enough. She'd expected him to argue. Or to show a rush of anger. To try, at least, to change her mind. He couldn't have, of course. She knew what she had to do, knew things were best handled this way.

Her mouth trembled, and she shot an enraged look at the closed door. After a moment, she lifted her chin, shrugged off her robe, stepped over it and strode into the bathroom.

"The hell with you, Mr. Romano," she whispered as she turned on the water in the shower. "Just—just the hell with—with…"

Tears rose in her eyes, spilled down her cheeks. She bowed her head under the spray and let them come.

"Susannah!"

She spun as the shower door opened. Matthew stood on the Italian tile floor. He was naked, furious and magnificently, fully male.

Susannah's heart turned over. She wanted to throw her arms around him, kiss him, tell him to get out of her life…

Instead, she did the only logical thing. She crossed her arms over herself in a gesture of classical feminine modesty.

"Are you crazy?" she demanded.

"One of us is," he said. "What kind of games are you playing, Madison?"

"I'm not playing games, Romano. And if you want to talk to me, you'll wait until—"

He stepped inside the shower stall, slammed the door after him and reached for her.

"Get out," she said. "Damn you, Romano…"

He pulled her into his arms and crushed her mouth beneath his. His kiss was rough and electric, and she struggled against it for a heartbeat before she moaned, sank her hands into his hair and opened her mouth to his. His hands slid down, cupped her bottom, lifted her. She wrapped her legs around him and he drove into her, fast and hard and deep, and she came at once, sobbing out his name against his lips, convulsing around him as he poured himself into her.

"Tell me you don't want that," he said, his voice hoarse and passionate in her ear.

"Matthew. Matthew, please…"

"Did you really think one night would be all I'd want, Susannah?"

"No. I don't… Oh. Oh, Matthew. I can't—I can't…"

"Yes," he said, pushing her against the marble wall. He was still inside her, hard again, swollen and hot. "Yes," he whispered, as he began moving, "you can. You will. We both will."

She shattered again, and cried out his name. He turned off the water, lifted her and carried her to bed, where he made sweet, tender love to her until she wept with joy in his arms.

In the end, they handled things with discretion.

He rose from the bed after they'd made love that last time, collected his clothes, kissed her lightly on the mouth and said he'd see her in an hour.

By the time the meeting began, the suite looked pristine. Matthew joined the little group a few minutes late.

"Sorry," he said pleasantly. "The traffic was heavier than I'd expected."

And if Susannah's heart beat faster at the sight of him, no one was the wiser.

The meeting ended. Everyone rose, stretched, got ready for work. The Sexiests huddled with Jimmy and Claire. The models—Bebe and Noelle today—huddled with the makeup guy and the hairdresser.

Matthew sought out Susannah.

"We should be finished by six," he said softly.

Susannah nodded. "I think so."

He turned his back to the room, blocking everyone from view. "I know a little bistro on the Left Bank." He smiled into her eyes. "Why don't I make reservations for eight o'clock?"

Susannah looked past his shoulder. "They're all watching us," she said in a breathless whisper.

"I'll come by at seven. We can have drinks first."

"Matthew, I don't—"

"Yes. You do." His eyes turned dark and smoky. "Shall I prove it to you the way I did this morning?"

Color flooded her face.

"Why?" she whispered.

He laughed, a low, sexy laugh that made her blood sizzle.

"I mean," she said quickly, "why me? I'm not your type."

"No," he said. He ran his finger along the back of her hand. Goose bumps rose on her skin. "You're not." He smiled again, right into her eyes. "You're not blond. You're not dumb—although many of the ladies I've dated would be very upset to hear you use that word in conjunction with them, Susie." His smile tilted. "I remember Miss North Carolina... She said she wanted to become a physicist."

"Matthew, I'm serious."

"So am I." His smile faded. "You're right. You're not my type. You're stubborn and hotheaded. You have a nasty temper and you like things your own way. "

"You're a fine one to talk," she said huffily.

"And I'd bet I'm not your type either, Madison. I don't think you like being with a man who reminds you that you're a woman."

"Your ego is unbearable, Romano."

"I'm just being honest." His eyes grew hot. "Tell me if Sam or Peter ever made you feel the way I make you feel."

Sam. And Peter. Oh, God...

"I can see the answer in your eyes, Susie." Matthew smiled. "Seven o'clock. Don't keep me waiting. I like my women to be prompt."

"I am not your—"

He bent his head and kissed her lightly on the mouth. Then he sauntered away.

Susannah stared around the room, trying to think of something to say. She wanted to murder him. The cat was out of the bag, for sure. Every eye was fixed on her. Claire was grinning, Jimmy was smiling, and Bebe looked as if she'd swallowed a shoehorn, but why wouldn't she? Bebe was tall and stunning, with legs up to her armpits and masses of blond hair down to her waist. Matthew's type, definitely.

But not anymore.

She was the woman Matthew wanted. She, and nobody else.

The sudden realization sent a flush of warmth through her blood. *Me,* she thought, *he wants me…*

And, in that moment, Susannah finally knew the truth.

She was deeply, completely in love with Matthew Romano.

They flew home late Sunday evening, Matthew to Los Angeles, Susannah to New York.

Her flight left first, and he waited with her at the airport.

It was silly, she knew, but she felt on the verge of tears. Already, the magical weekend seemed to have taken place in the distant past. Every time she looked at Matthew, she was afraid she was going to blurt out something she would regret, like those foolish, dangerous words, *I love you.*

So she talked, nonstop, about business. The next issue of the magazine and The Sexiest Man Alive issue, which would come out Valentine's Day. Matthew teased her, gently, about which of the Sexiests she'd choose to be the centerfold.

"The only sexy guy I want you to think about is me," he said, softly enough so no one could hear but with a look in his eyes that made her body flush with remembered heat.

She wanted to tell him the truth, that he really was the sexiest man alive and that she loved him. Instead, she talked about circulation figures and advertising revenues until, finally, her flight was called.

"Goodbye," she said.

Matthew tugged her into his arms and kissed her, gently at first, then passionately. Any last hopes she'd harbored about keeping their relationship a secret were gone.

"You shouldn't have done that," she said shakily, when he lifted his mouth from hers.

"They all know, Susie," he said, with a little smile. "They can see it in your face, and in mine." He tucked a stray curl behind her ear, his fingers lingering on her cheek. "I have to be in L.A. all week, but I'll fly to New York on Friday. Okay?"

How will I live without you until Friday? she thought, but she wasn't foolish enough to say that.

"That's fine," she said, and smiled. "I'll be busy all week, anyway. Even if you managed to fly in, I wouldn't have time to see you.''

His smile seemed to dim. ''Business is business.''

''Exactly.''

''You'd better make sure you're not busy on Friday,'' he said gruffly.

She knew he was going to kiss her again, so she didn't give him the chance. ''Until Friday,'' she said, and she broke away and hurried to the boarding gate.

CHAPTER TWELVE

THE week seemed interminable. She couldn't believe it could take so long to get from Monday to Friday.

But Friday came and went.

Matthew phoned. He was apologetic, but business...

"I know," Susannah said. "You don't have to explain."

He sent flowers and more flowers. He sent chocolates. The flowers were lovely. Peter thought so, too, and neatly beheaded them all. Susannah swept up the mess and told herself there was nothing meaningful in the sight of those sad little corpses lying among the coffee grounds in the kitchen trash.

"Next Friday, for certain," Matthew said, when she called to thank him for the flowers. But as soon as she heard his voice the following Wednesday, she knew.

"Can't make it, hmm?" Her words shimmered with artificial cheer.

"Susannah." He sounded hurried. She could imagine him glancing at his watch while he spoke with her. "Susannah, I'm sorry. I really thought I'd be able to get to New York this weekend."

"That's all right, Matthew. I have plans anyway."

"Plans?" He sounded brusque. "What kind of plans?"

"Oh," she said gaily, "just plans." Peter leaped onto the counter and butted his head against her hand. "With—with an old friend."

"An old friend?"

"Yes," she said. "Goodbye, Matthew."

She hung up the phone. He'd sounded more than brusque, he'd sounded curt. She might have expected that.

She lifted Peter into her arms and kissed the top of his head. Matthew didn't like the idea of her having a life that didn't include him, even if the magic of Paris had worn off in the reality of San Francisco. He didn't want to continue the relationship. Or maybe he did, but on more convenient terms. Business was business. Sex was sex.

"Of course," she said.

And, really, no surprise. She wasn't important enough to put before other things.

Tears filled her eyes, rolled down her cheeks. Peter blinked when they plunked onto his head.

"Mrrow," he said indignantly, and demanded she put him down. Even he was deserting her.

"Even you, Petey, " Susannah said, and then she slid down the wall, covered her face with her hands and wept.

In Los Angeles, Matthew slammed down the phone, tilted back his chair and glowered at his brother.

"She's seeing somebody," he said.

Joe looked up from the report he'd been reading. "Who's seeing somebody?"

"The woman spends the weekend in bed with me and not two weeks later, she's seeing somebody else!"

"What woman? What bed? What are you talking about, Matt?"

Matthew sat up straight. "Susannah, that's what. I know she doesn't confuse sex with—with anything more than sex, but damn, you'd think she'd put a little more value on that weekend."

"Susannah? Our Susannah? You and she—"

"Yeah," Matthew growled. "And she's not 'our' Susannah. She's..."

"Yes?" Joe said, with an interested smile.

Matthew shot to his feet. "It was meaningless. We were in Paris. It happened, that's all."

Joe's brows rose. "Paris? I thought you and the French chick... Baby?"

"Bebe," Matthew said, and shuddered. "Don't tell me she called again."

"She's been lighting up the switchboard," Joe said, and chuckled. "You should be flattered, Matt. It's not every day a woman follows a guy across the ocean."

"She followed her career. She's got a modeling gig here,

so she's playing all her cards. She left a dozen messages at my hotel in Paris. Now that she's here, she's driving me nuts. The other day, she pounced as I was coming out of the office."

Joe grinned. "Poor Matt. Women just throw themselves at his feet. So, in Paris, it wasn't the French babe, it was our... Sorry. It was Susannah, huh?"

"You could say that, yes."

"Why not the French babe?"

"She's not my type."

"What's she look like? Maybe she's my type."

"She looks the way they all look," Matthew said impatiently. "Tall, gorgeous face, great body, eager to please, blond hair down to her butt..."

"Ah," Joe said wisely. "Definitely not your type."

Matthew scowled. "I know. It's crazy. The one who's really not my type is Susannah. In looks, in temperament... The woman has the disposition of a porcupine."

"Is that why you were supposed to fly to New York last weekend? To see her?"

Matthew nodded.

"But you canceled out. And now you've canceled again."

"Business," Matthew said gruffly. "The Vernon deal, the Tolland contract..."

"Oh. Well, sure. Any of that stuff would be more important than being with the lady."

"Don't be ridiculous. Nothing's more important than..." Matthew muttered under his breath. "You see what I mean? It's crazy."

"You want to see Susannah?"

"No."

"You want to break things off."

"No!" Matthew jammed his hands into his trouser pockets and paced the length of his office. "You know how it is, Joey. You meet a woman, something clicks, you know where it's going to lead."

"Of course. Straight to bed."

"Right. Once you get there...well, no matter how great it is, you know it's going to end. But..."

"But?"

There was a long silence. "But this situation doesn't seem to be going that way."

"I don't understand."

"Hell," Matthew said, with a bitter laugh, "neither do I."

Joe cleared his throat. "I must be missing something here. Susannah doesn't look like your dream girl. She's as bristly as a porcupine."

"You've got it."

"So what's the problem?"

Matthew stared at his brother. It was a good question. What, exactly, *was* the problem?

Joey smiled. "You know what you need, pal? A night on the town. A couple of hot chicks, some good vino, a rare steak. Take Dr. Romano's advice, you'll be a new man in the morning."

Matthew smiled, too. "You think?"

"I know. And, if you change your mind and decide you still want to see Susannah, well, she'll be there when you want her."

"Yeah." Matthew cleared his throat. "I just wonder about this friend she's seeing this weekend."

"Did you ask her who it was?"

"No."

"Why not?"

"It's none of my business."

"Well, then…"

"It better not be Sam. Or Peter."

"Who?"

"On the other hand, we didn't make any commitments. If she wants to see another guy, that's that."

"Now you're thinking straight." Joe clapped Matt on the back. "Take out your little black book. Get yourself a date for tonight. I'm seeing somebody new, did I tell you? We'll go out to dinner, have some laughs…"

Matthew shook his head. "Thanks, but I'm not really in the mood."

"Nonsense. You need a night on the town." Joe's voice softened. "Matt. You need to clear your head, and this is the only way to do it."

"Maybe," Matthew said. "But I'm going to pass."

*   *   *

Things started to come apart at *CHIC* on Friday morning.

Claire came bristling into Susannah's office at nine o'clock and dumped a stack of magazines on her desk.

"Time for the monthly check," she said briskly. "Got to see what the competition's up to."

"You see. I'm busy."

"Busy?" Claire's brows rose. "You're staring into space."

"I'm being creative," Susannah said stubbornly. "How's the vote coming? Who's going to be our sexiest man center-fold?"

Claire grinned. "Actually, there's an unofficial but unanimous vote for Matthew. "

Susannah could think of other names for him, but she decided to keep them to herself.

"The man is gorgeous, Suze." Claire smiled slyly. "Studly, to quote an authority."

"Claire, I'm really busy. Could we get to work? Let's see what's doing in these magazines."

Claire raised an eyebrow but said nothing. Instead, she shoved the current issue of *Vogue* across the desk.

Susannah opened it, thumbed quickly through the glossy pages.

"Nice idea they have with this layout on shoes. Ask Amy what she thinks. Next?"

"*Harper's*. Take a look at the perfume ad on page eighty. Why don't we see if we can't get some bigger advertising bucks out of Chanel?"

"Fine. Next?"

"The latest *Women's Wear Daily*. There's a really clever column on… What's the matter?"

Susannah didn't answer. She sat staring at a page of celebrity snapshots.

"Suze?" Claire came behind the desk. "You're white as a ghost. What… Oh, hell. Is that—"

"Matthew." Susannah swallowed. "Matthew and—"

"Bebe. The model."

Bebe, the model. Bebe and Matthew, on the steps of a building the caption identified as the headquarters of Romano Inc., in California. Bebe, with her pouty mouth, her big eyes, her long blond hair. Bebe, standing a step above Matthew, her hands on his shoulders, her big eyes gazing adoringly into his face. And Matthew, gazing back at her, his hands spanning her waist, the look on his face one of dark intensity.

"The sexiest bachelor alive," the caption burbled, "and his newest conquest, the hot new model Bebe Le Beau."

Susannah began to tremble. "The son of a bitch," she whispered.

Claire tried to tug the magazine from her hands. "Maybe it's not him. Maybe it's not her. Maybe—"

"The no-account, lying, cheating swine!"

"Suze, there's got to be an explanation."

"There's an explanation, all right. I just gave it to you. Matthew Romano is a pig. A filthy, lowlife, dirty pig. And I'm a fool. Was a fool. Was..."

Susannah grabbed the telephone and punched a button.

"Suze? Listen, you really need to calm down. Think this through. Don't do anything you'll—"

"I want to speak to Matthew Romano," Susannah said furiously. "This is Susannah Madison calling."

"Suze," Claire pleaded, "don't do this!"

"Don't do what?" Susannah slapped her hand over the receiver. "Recover what little remains of my dignity? We've been friends for a long time, Claire. Don't ruin it by defending a—a gob of human scum!"

"I'm not defending him. I'm just saying you could be making a mistake."

"I made my mistake in Paris. And now I'm going to set things right."

Matthew's secretary came on the line at the same instant Claire shut the door behind her.

"He's not in?" Susannah said. "Not to me, you mean. No, there's no problem. Just give him a message, please." She took a deep breath. "Tell Mr. Romano that he has my notice. That's right. I'm quitting. Quitting as of today. No, he won't be able to return my call. I'm leaving the office immediately, and I won't be taking any calls at home." She hesitated, then went on in angry defiance, despite the tears that were already blurring her vision. "Tell him I'm spending the weekend with—with my lover. With Mr. Peter Katz. And Mr. Katz and I most definitely will not want to be disturbed."

Susannah slammed down the telephone, gathered her things and left.

Peter didn't like wine. He didn't like beer, either. He was pretty much a heavy cream man.

But he was wild about anchovies, so that was how Susannah ordered the pizza. One large, extra cheese, mushrooms and onions on one half, anchovies on the other.

The wine and the beer, which she'd bought on the way home, she kept for herself.

The only problem was, she never drank much of either. So she stared at the six-pack of Rolling Rock and at the bottle of Chianti and tried to decide which would go better with pizza and with her plans for the evening.

What would a woman drink if she were dining with her lover by candlelight? If she were wearing her very oldest jeans, her most faded sweatshirt, a pair of wool socks...and if she had a photograph of Matthew Romano pinned to a dartboard? That had been her other purchase, made on the way home, and it was going to be, she was certain, the most rewarding.

Susannah lit the candles, opened the wine and poured herself a glass.

"To you," she said, and hurled a dart at the board. It hit right in the middle of Matthew's studly face. "Good shot," she said happily, and raised her glass in salute. Matthew looked decidedly uncomfortable with a dart in his forehead and his hands outstretched, clasping nothing but air because, of course, she'd snipped out Bebe and consigned her to the trash basket, where she belonged.

She took a sip of the wine. It wasn't very good. She'd bought it because of its cute raffia basket, which did not seem to be a very useful means of selection.

The beer, then. She dug in the utility drawer, found an opener, wrenched off the bottle top and lifted the bottle to her lips. Yes, that was better. Now, if she could only get enough of it down to get plastered, she'd be happy.

This was an evening she was going to remember. She was going to pig out on pizza because, even with anchovies on

top, Peter would never eat more than half a slice. She was
going to throw darts at Romano's studly face until it was obliterated. And she was going to get drunk enough to fall into
bed and sleep the night through without once staring at the
ceiling and trying to figure out why in hell she'd ever imagined herself in love with a lowlife, double-dealing fink like
Matthew because, it went without saying, she was not in love
with him and never had been.

"You're pathetic," she said.

Peter looked at her and meowed. Susannah bent and lifted
him in her arms.

"No, not you, Petey. I'm the one who's pathetic. You'd
think, considering the times we live in, a woman wouldn't
have to lie to herself in order to go to bed with a man. I wanted
to sleep with Matthew. Why couldn't I have done it without
all that love nonsense?"

Peter purred and licked her chin.

"I suppose, in a way, I owe Mr. Romano a favor. If I hadn't
seen that picture of him and the FDB..."

"Mrrow?"

"The French Dumb Blonde. If I hadn't seen that, I'd have
sighed over him for another couple of weeks. And what an
absolute waste of time that would have been."

"Mrrow," Peter said, and shut his eyes.

"I just feel badly for Claire and the others. But they'll be
fine. The next issues of *CHIC* are all set and, let's face it,
Petey, we both know that our Mr. Romano's going to dump
the magazine, no matter what its advertising numbers or its
circulation. He just set the whole scheme up so he could..."

So he could what? Seduce her? Susannah tilted the bottle
to her lips again. Romano was a rat but, as he'd always said,
business was business. He wouldn't have spent all that money
just to get her into bed. Besides, he wouldn't have had to.
She'd have ended up in bed with him anyway if he'd just
persisted. His kisses had turned her knees liquid. Oh, those
kisses...

The doorbell rang.

Susannah gave herself a little shake. "Dinner," she said
brightly, as she undid the door locks. "Petey, you're in for a

treat. Anchovies, and you'll get a little visit with your old friend, the pizza delivery..."

Oh, God!

It wasn't the pizza delivery man. It was Matthew. Matthew, wearing jeans and those hiking boots, a sweatshirt that didn't look much newer than hers, the beat-up leather jacket and a look that seemed dangerous enough to kill.

"Surprised to see me, Madison?"

Susannah tried to come up with a response. Peter, who didn't like strangers, was humming to himself and backing onto her shoulder, using four-paw, all-claw drive.

"What—what are you doing here, Romano?"

Matthew smiled coldly. "You walked out in the middle of an expensive project. Did you really think I wouldn't react?"

"React all you like. I handed in my resignation."

"You told my secretary you were quitting. That's not exactly a professional way to hand in a resignation."

"Sue me," Susannah said. "And now, if you don't mind—"

Matthew brushed past her and slammed the door shut. "I don't have to sue you. Do you really think you'll ever get another decent job in publishing once this story gets out?"

He was right. It was something she hadn't thought of, but even if she had, she'd have made that phone call and marched out of that office.

"I'll find a job in something else, then," she said. "Get out of my apartment, Romano. You're not welcome... Where are you going?"

"Mrrow," Peter said at the sound of her raised voice. He leaped from her shoulder onto the couch as Susannah stalked after Matthew, who was poking his nose into her bedroom.

"Charming place," he said politely.

"It's *my* place," Susannah said in warning. "You have no right to—"

"Cozy," he said, peering into the tiny kitchen. "Dinner for two, complete with candles." His brows lifted. "Wine and beer? You and Mr. Katz plan on drinking a lot tonight?"

"Me and..." Susannah flushed. "Peter—Peter wasn't sure which he'd prefer with—with our meal. So I bought both."

"Ah." Matthew strolled toward the table, lifted her glass

of wine and took a sniff. "Nasty stuff," he said, with a shudder. "But the beer's a good choice."

Susannah's legs felt rubbery. He was going to look at the counter and see the dartboard propped against the wall any minute. She edged in front of it while her brain ran in circles, trying to figure a way to get him out of the room.

"Where is Mr. Katz, by the way? I'd like to meet him."

"He's—he's in the bathroom."

"Wasn't that the bathroom I passed in the hall? The door was open. It looked empty to me."

Susannah swallowed dryly. "I forgot. He—he went down to—to put another quarter in the meter. His car's parked out front."

"Well, that shouldn't take long." Matthew folded his arms, propped a hip against the edge of the table. "I'll wait."

"Are you dense, Romano? I didn't invite you in, and I'm sure not inviting you to—"

"Mrrow?"

Peter strolled into the room, tail high.

"Nice cat." Matthew squatted and held out his hand. "Strange, I didn't see him the other time I was here."

"He keeps a low profile when strangers are around. He doesn't like..." Susannah gave an inward groan as Peter offered Matthew his head to scratch.

"Yeah, well, he seems to like me."

"That's only because he doesn't know you." Susannah put her hands on her hips. "Give him time."

Matthew picked up the cat. "That's the general idea, Madison. By the time Katz gets back, this guy and I will be old pals. What's his name?"

"His name? His name is—is Fluffy."

"Fluffy? For a cat with such dignity?" Matthew rubbed Peter between the ears. "You have my sympathies, fella."

"Look, Romano. I—I understand that you're upset."

"Upset? Do I look upset?"

"Peeved, then."

"There's a word I can't stand, Madison. Real men do not get peeved."

"Oh, for God's sake, will you just get out of here? My—Peter will be angry if he finds you."

"Mrrow?" Peter said.

Matthew grinned wolfishly. "That's good to hear. You think he'll take a poke at me when I tell him he's got one hell of a nerve, moving in on my woman?"

"Your…?"

"That's right. My woman." Matthew put Peter on the table and strode toward her. "I have a rule I live by, Susie."

"Don't call me that."

"It's a simple rule." He reached out and clasped her shoulders. "I'm faithful to the woman I'm involved with. And I expect her to be faithful to me."

"Ha," Susannah said, and folded her arms.

"We became lovers in Paris. Didn't that mean anything to you?"

"We slept together, Romano."

"Yeah. So you kept telling me." He shook her, not hard but not gently, either. "Call it what you like, Susannah. I expected fidelity."

Susannah pulled free of his grasp. "Fidelity? You?" She laughed. "You don't know… What's the matter?"

"What in hell is that on the sink?"

She turned quickly, snatched the dartboard and put it behind her. "It's nothing."

"It sure looks like something to me. Hand it over."

"No," she huffed, as he reached for the board. "Romano, don't you dare!"

Matthew wrenched the dartboard from her hand. "I don't believe it," he said, as he stared at his mutilated photo. "Where'd you get this?"

"What's the difference?"

"This damn photo was in last Sunday's *San Francisco Post*."

"Well, you made the big time, Romano. It ran in *Women's Wear Daily,* too."

Matthew looked up, his eyes narrowed. "Is that what this is all about? Did you think I was cheating on you?"

"No. Of course not. Why would I care if you were seeing Bebe and Claudia and Claudette and Noelle and—and half the blondes on two continents?" Susannah tossed her head. "Your life is your own, Romano. You can do what you like."

"You did think I was cheating." Matthew tossed the dart-board aside. "And you decided to get even by getting engaged to Peter Katz."

"Merroww," Peter said, and wove gracefully between Matthew's ankles.

"You are some piece of work, Madison. I don't even know this guy Peter—"

"Meow?"

"And I sure as hell don't like him, but not even Peter—"

"Mrrrow."

"Listen, Fluffy," Matthew said, glaring at his ankles, "I like you a lot. But you sure have an awful lot to say, for a—"

The doorbell rang. Susannah didn't move.

"Your lover, I believe. Aren't you going to let him in?" Matthew's eyes grew dark. "Or does he have a key?"

The bell rang again. Matthew lifted one eyebrow, picked up the cat and headed for the living room with Susannah running after him.

"No," she said, "wait."

Matthew opened the door.

"Hi."

The pizza delivery man beamed at them both.

"Got a pizza here for you, Suze," he said, giving her a little wave, which she feebly returned. "And, of course, for Peter."

"Charming," Matthew said, with a killer smile. "You know them both, I see."

"Oh, yeah. Sure. Suze orders in once a week. Always the same. Extra cheese all round, mushrooms and onions on one half, anchovies on the other."

Matthew gave a visible shudder. "Anchovies on pizza?"

"Yeah, I know, but some folks like it that way." The delivery man grinned. "And Petey here loves his anchovies." He reached out, and Peter permitted himself to be petted. "Don't you, Peter, old man?"

There was a resounding silence. Matthew stiffened, turned and stared at Susannah. She tossed her head, spun on her heel and marched into the kitchen.

She was pouring her glass of wine down the sink by the time she heard the door close and then the sound of his footsteps. If she could just get through the next few moments with some semblance of dignity…

"Madison." Matthew's hand fell on her shoulder.

"It's my business, not yours, and I'm not going to explain."

Matthew turned her around. His expression was unreadable. "And Sam? Is there a parakeet involved in this, too?"

She couldn't help it. She laughed, and for one second, Matthew seemed to laugh, too. But then his face became inscrutable again, and so did hers.

"Sam is an old friend," she said evenly, because what was the sense in lying? "We went to high school together. I see him whenever I go home to visit my mother. He's smart, he's funny, and I adore him." She licked her lips. "And he's gay."

Matthew nodded. "Two men in your life. One gay and the other one…" He looked at Peter, lying contentedly in his arms, smiled a little and set the cat gently on the kitchen table. "Neutered?"

Susannah blushed. "I know this is all very amusing, Romano, but—"

Matthew bent his head and kissed her mouth. "I'm tempted to turn you over my knee and spank the daylights out of you, Madison," he said gently.

"You just try it," Susannah sputtered. "Because if you dare—if you dare… Why did you kiss me just now, Romano? If you really think you're going to get me to—to sleep with you after the runaround you've given me the past two weeks, after knowing you've been waltzing around with—with that— that French piece of…"

Matthew grinned. "Careful, sweetheart. You don't want say anything you'll regret." He cupped her face with his hands, tilted it to his. "And you're wrong. I don't want you to sleep with me. I want you to make love with me."

"As if there were a difference," Susannah said in a shaky voice.

"There's one hell of a difference, Madison, and you know it. A man and a woman make love when they're in love." His smile tilted and became so soft and sweet that she feared it might break her heart. "And that's our situation, sweetheart. I love you, and you love me, and we certainly almost mucked things up, big time."

"Oh, Matthew," she whispered, "we certainly almost did."

Matthew put his arms around Susannah and kissed her. A long time later, he lifted his head and looked into her eyes.

"There's nothing between Bebe and me. She came on to me in Paris—she got it into her head I was some hotshot director and that I could get her a screen test. She's here on some kind of modeling assignment, and she's been turning up like a bad penny. That photo was taken by some paparazzo. Bebe was waiting for me outside my office. The guy got a shot of me telling her to back off."

Susannah let out a long sigh. "I thought—I know it's awful, but I really believed..."

"It's my fault you did. I knew I loved you in Paris. I think I knew it the first minute I saw you. But I've been a bachelor for years, sweetheart." He smiled into her eyes. "The thought of getting down on one knee and asking you to be my wife struck terror into my heart."

Susannah's eyes glittered. "Are you proposing to me, Romano?"

"Yes, if you'll have me. I know we'll have details to work out. Your career—here at *CHIC,* I mean—but..."

She rose on her toes and kissed his mouth.

"People read on the coast, don't they?" she said, with a breathless laugh. "There are magazines in L.A., and publishing companies, too. It's time I found a new challenge."

Matthew felt like a man who'd just realized he'd spent the past two weeks holding his breath.

"Is that a yes?"

Susannah smiled. "Of course it is. I adore you, Matthew Romano. I love you with all my heart. Sex isn't just sex, not when you're in love."

"No," he said. He kissed her again and then he flashed a wicked smile. "It's spectacular."

"Mmm." Susannah sighed as he slid his hands under her sweatshirt. "To think I'm going to have the sexiest man alive all to myself."

Matthew swung her into his arms. "Hold that thought, Susie," he whispered, and kissed her.

Peter watched them disappear inside the bedroom.

"Mrrow," he said, and trotted into the living room to see

about opening the pizza box. There were anchovies to be had, and lots of them, which was a darned good thing, because it looked as if his people were going to be busy for a very, very long time.

EPILOGUE

●

CHIC-CHAT

Dear Readers:
It's been wonderful, working together these past months, to shape *CHIC* into a magazine that speaks for women like us. I'm going to miss our chats on this page, just as I'm going to miss all of you who have become my friends, but it's time for me to move on and leave *CHIC* in the capable hands of your new editor-in-chief, Claire Haines. We've shared a lot, you and I. Together, we found the sexiest places to have dinner, the sexiest getaway hotels and the sexiest men alive. Well, I'm going to share something else with you. It's a secret I suspect many of you already know.
Sex is wonderful. But love, and romance, are the things that make us truly happy.
By the time you read this, I'll be married to a man I love with all my heart. I'd like to invite you to share one last moment with me. If you turn to this month's centerfold, you'll see our wedding picture.
I ask you, ladies, isn't my guy gorgeous?

With love always,

Susannah
Susannah Madison Romano

Passion

Looking for stories that *sizzle?* Wanting a read that has a little extra *spice?*

Harlequin Presents® is thrilled to bring you romances that turn up the heat!

In March 1999 look out for:

The Marriage Surrender by Michelle Reid

Harlequin Presents #2014

Every other month throughout 1999, there'll be a **PRESENTS PASSION** book by one of your favorite authors: Miranda Lee, Helen Bianchin, Sara Craven and Michelle Reid!

*Pick up a **PRESENTS PASSION**— where **seduction** is guaranteed!*

Available wherever Harlequin books are sold.

HARLEQUIN®
Makes any time special ™

Coming Next Month

HARLEQUIN PRESENTS®

THE BEST HAS JUST GOTTEN BETTER!

#2013 CONTRACT BABY Lynne Graham
(The Husband Hunters)
Becoming a surrogate mother was Polly's only option when her mother needed a life-saving operation. But the baby's father was businessman Raul Zaforteza, and he would do anything to keep his unborn child—even marry Polly....

#2014 THE MARRIAGE SURRENDER Michelle Reid
(Presents Passion)
When Joanna had no choice but to turn to her estranged husband, Sandro, for help, he agreed, but on one condition: that she return to his bed—as his wife. But what would happen when he discovered her secret?

#2015 THE BRIDE WORE SCARLET Diana Hamilton
When Daniel Faber met his stepbrother's mistress, Annie Kincaid, he decided the only way he could keep her away from his stepbrother was to kidnap her! But the plan had a fatal flaw—Daniel had realized he wanted Annie for himself!

#2016 DANTE'S TWINS Catherine Spencer
(Expecting!)
It wasn't just jealous colleagues who believed Leila was marrying for money; so did her boss, and fiancé Dante Rossi! How could Leila marry him without convincing him she was more than just the mother of his twins?

#2017 ONE WEDDING REQUIRED! Sharon Kendrick
(Wanted: One Wedding Dress)
Amber was delighted to be preparing to marry her boss, hunky Finn Fitzgerald. But after she gave an ill-advised interview to an unscrupulous journalist, it seemed there wasn't going to be a wedding at all....

#2018 MISSION TO SEDUCE Sally Wentworth
Allie was certain she didn't need bodyguard Drake Marsden for her assignment in Russia. But Drake refused to leave her day or night, and then he decided that the safest place for her was in his bed!